Joe Stepped Off The Train
and other stories

compiled by Steven Kay

IN SUPPORT OF

WAR

child

1889books

JOE STEPPED OFF THE TRAIN and other stories

First published in 2016 by 1889 books

All author royalties being donated to War Child

www.1889books.co.uk

ISBN: 978-0-9935762-0-1

War Child

War Child aims to provide sustainable, intensive support to the most marginalised and vulnerable children and young people in conflict-affected parts of the world — not just providing aid but strengthening the capacity of the families, communities and authorities to look after their own children.

Their projects are all rooted in local communities: involving and employing local people. For example, their child protection committees bring together local councillors, policemen, teachers, tribal elders etc. to train them to take responsibility for identifying and protecting vulnerable children in their communities. The best kind of project is one that will be continued by local people afterwards.

Education is a big focus in the majority of War Child's projects because in countries affected by conflict an education is not only life-changing (giving a child basic literacy skills opens up all sorts of opportunities), but can also be life-saving (teaching a child how to avoid land-mines). It is not just about getting children into schools (which during conflict can sometimes be unsafe), but enabling them to learn, whatever their circumstances and environment. This includes things like providing informal education and training programmes; for example, for children who can't travel into school during times of violence or those who have been pulled into the violence themselves as child-soldiers and need to catch-up on their lost education or learn a vocation.

Introduction

This collection started life a few years ago following a short story competition at work that Elizabeth Thomas and I entered. Entries had to have one of three given starting lines, one of which was: "Joe stepped off the train…" *A Mother's Love* was the winner: the first short story I had written since school in the 1970s. *Home* came third. It was interesting how both of us had chosen the same starting line and both had gone for war themes. I contacted Elizabeth to say how much I liked *Home* and that I thought it better than the second placed story. Elizabeth made the suggestion that we should write some more, get them published and then read out on Radio 4. I had to rein her back a little from that surge of enthusiasm and ambition and suggested baby-steps: that we could perhaps get some stories together first and see what it looked like.

So we started a short story conversation: e-mailing our stories to each other for comment and criticism, editing and re-editing as we went. It confirmed that we had similar tastes when it came to stories. Our relationship has developed through the stories—though we've still not actually met (we work for a national organisation).

We eventually ran out of steam, or ideas, or time and didn't progress beyond the initial nine stories.

I picked the idea back up in the summer of 2015 with the plan of making it into a charity fundraiser for War Child as all our stories were about war: how it affects people and changes lives, so what better charity? I put out an appeal through social media and my blog and so started collecting the additional stories. The intention was that they would all start with the same line, but writers are a wilful bunch and I soon realised I would end up rejecting great stories for the sake of dogma — hence the: "and other stories."

It has been great working with these writers putting the collection together — I love the diversity of stories but also how there is a coherence to the collection. The authors have all been very patient with me — taking my, sometimes pedantic, suggestions for edits in good spirit. I hope that process has resulted in a collection that is better as a result of that collaborative approach.

Some of the writers are setting out on their writing career — others have been at it for a long time. The stories are the result of many hours of work by each writer — each of whom has given their time freely. I hope you will appreciate the outcome and if you enjoy the particular stories you will seek out the writer's other work and support them by reading their work.

However, more important than supporting us is supporting War Child. All author royalties go to War Child. Please review it on Amazon and Goodreads, please blog and tweet about it, and please buy it for your friends and help to support this superb organisation and the children they support. Many thanks.

Steven Kay, 2016

Addendum by Elizabeth Thomas: I am honoured to have my work be a part of this collection. A complete amateur and novice, I had used writing to scratch a creative itch over the years from time to time but before submitting *Home* I had never entered a competition or given my writing to anyone else to read. I am so pleased that my initial enthusiasm to develop this project, although maybe a little ambitious, planted a seed with Steve and that he has been tenacious enough to get this collection together. This project is proof that from small ideas big things can grow and this is demonstrated no better than in the work done every day by the amazing War Child charity.

Contents

A Mother's Love

Joe stepped off the train and held the package close to his side. He adjusted his weight on his crutch and dropped his kit bag to the platform. It smelt like home – the grease and steam from the engine mixed with that distinct smell of man, beast and machine working flat out to produce shells and armour plate. And yet there was no joy in him.

Mick's mother lived in the notorious Crofts; he would take a cab from the front of the station: people moved aside, a look of horror mixed with pity in their eyes. Before he could attempt to rebuild his life he had to give her this – all that was left of Mick wrapped in, now smutted, brown paper – Christ! how was he going to explain to her. The Christmas table at Mick's would have a very empty seat. Good ol' Mick – what a bloody laugh they'd had last year – as he lost his last Christmas dinner over the side in the Bay of Biscay. Sailing to Egypt was just one big adventure then for boys who, until they'd enlisted, had never been further than Derby that happy September day in times of innocence when the United netted five.

The old horse strained to move the cab away – all the good ones had been blown to bits in France. Town looked just the same, and yet everything had changed. He fingered the string on the packet – Mick's book – his Bible – his lucky charm – with a sniper's bullet right through the middle of it. What sort of God was this? As he'd lain there next to Mick he felt warm liquid seeping over his own chest – he'd been hit too. Except, when he'd felt inside, it was just his pewter flask leaking whisky where it had been punctured by shrapnel. The bloody irony of that! The sweet boy who'd taken the pledge, shot dead through his

1

holy book, and the sinner saved by his sin.

Ten minutes before Zero on the first of July they'd left
the trench, comrades side by side, as the mortars opened
up a hurricane bombardment and a huge mine exploded to
the south shattering the world and sending smoke and
earth hundreds of feet into the sky, drowning out even the
deafening noise of the bombardment. There they'd lain
down in the middle of No Man's Land as grenades and
artillery flew over. Then it went quiet, momentarily –
perhaps it wouldn't happen after all? But Zero had arrived
– the artillery started again and the whistles blew. They got
to their feet – they had to walk with rifles raised, not run –
and then all of hell descended. They were supposed to be
going forward but didn't: as the front line fell more targets
took their place, bodies piled up and blood and humanity
mixed with mud. Screams and moans and cries of
"mother" from boys only just in breeches pierced through
the din, the smoke, the blasts that shook and rent flesh.
Him and Mick pushed on but the bloody wire was still
there and they couldn't cross the last few yards. Then
Mick fell and he'd picked him up and dragged him towards
a shell hole – then a grenade went off and he came round
with Mick under him and a searing pain in his foot and
across the side of his face. Mick was conscious; he tried to
keep him talking but gradually he had faded in his arms.
He kissed him, but he had never known just how much he
meant to him. How could he ever?

There were a few of the Pals in that shell hole. They'd
had to fight like hell to defend that open grave until
nightfall. Then he'd had to leave Mick – along with all the
others they stepped over on their way back. All he could
return of Mick was that precious Bible – the one with
pressed poppies and wild flowers in.

He had been amongst the one in three of the City Battalion that survived that day.

He was shipped out to a first aid station and was spared those next three nightmare days clearing up the mess. He had tried to find out if Mick's body had been retrieved and buried – he couldn't bear to think of that beautiful boy – out there – being stripped by rats and maggots.

The next day the post from home arrived and they were instructed to open it all – cigarettes, chocolates, socks, packed up with tender cards, letters of good wishes and prayers sent out to a God who just wasn't there.

No afterlife. Just this. One go at getting it right.

No post arrived for Mick, for which he was grateful.

He tried to give the cabbie the one and six but he refused it – always that look in their eyes – he'd rather have their respect. He stood and looked round for the right courtyard. A child stood gawping at him.

'Nah den kid, weer's Mick Flannery's 'ouse?'

The child, bare-footed and wearing clothes his own mother wouldn't have considered fit for cleaning cloths, led him timidly into a soot-blackened courtyard. There was a stench of overflowing middens; some hens pecking near an open drain and the broken paving was coated in brown slime. He shuddered as his mind flashed back to July. His hand went up to the claret scar on his cheek. The boy indicated the house; Joe tossed him a ha'penny and approached the door. He took a deep breath and knocked. A girl pulled the door open, something in those blue eyes said she was Mick's sister – how could he not know? – but Mick never spoke of his family.

'Yeah?'

'Is Mrs Flannery in?'

'Mother there's a fella at t' doo-er'

'What's 'e want?' came a voice from inside.

'I dunno.'

Joe waited. A dishevelled woman came out of the gloom. She was filthy; grey, matted hair; ancient-looking. Joe thought she had been drinking.

'I'm looking for Mrs Flannery – Michael's mother.'

'Tha's found 'er.' Joe was shocked. This woman could surely never have given birth to someone so beautiful.

'I'm a friend of Mick's.' He held out the package. 'This was his Bible. I think he might have wanted you to have it.'

'Tha can keep it. I'm not bothered.'

The door closed in his face. He didn't move. She was supposed to invite him in, ask how Mick died, weep and wail.

How could a mother's love be less than his own?

Home

Joe stepped off the train and held the package close to his side. The big, round man he'd been sitting next to rudely bumped past him sending the gas mask box round his neck swinging. He didn't even say sorry. Joe stood rigid on the platform not quite knowing what to do next. He hugged the brown paper package in his arms and inhaled deeply as his insides felt all funny. The familiar smell of mummy's perfume brought sharply into his mind thoughts of the home he'd left behind. The shiny front step, patent black in the rain, the soft, rag rug in front of the fireplace a million shades of blue, the noise of her gentle singing, humming when she didn't know the words, the smells of baking from the little warm kitchen. Tears wobbled at the corners of his eyes as his thoughts had him curled like a baby rabbit in her lap, the wireless gently rambling and his short blond hair being softly stroked, over and over until he felt so drowsy.

'Yes. Over here. Come on. Yoo hoo. Over here.'

Joe snapped back to the confusion of the platform, other children, some with suitcases, some with string-tied parcels like him, some holding teddies or dolls, all of them with gas masks round their necks and all labelled like parcels.

'Come on dearie, you're with me. Come on, over here. Off we go,' called the pink-faced lady in the flowery dress as she pointed with her clipboard and strode out of the station. Joe followed on behind three other children, obedient chicks after a mother hen.

He wasn't quite the smallest. The little girl with the ginger curls was still a little tot; she sat with the pink-faced lady and sucked her thumb. Daddy had told him before he walked away, tall and straight in his uniform, that he needed Joe to be brave, be the man of the house, and so now sucking his thumb was only for bedtime, only when he was alone in the dark under the covers. And he had been brave. He had managed to smile when she'd left him at Kings Cross and agreed how exciting an adventure it would be, like a holiday. What a big boy he had been when he had seen, through the steam, her sad face trying to smile to cover up her crying as the train began to move.

Joe knew there was a time, before Daddy went away for so long, a time when everything was safe and well and people didn't worry so much about Germans and bombs, but like the faint memory of a dream come the light of morning, he couldn't quite remember enough to know how it felt. He had played happily on the broken-down houses, bits of mangled window frames becoming machine guns, loose bricks built into bunkers. He almost knew no different but he had noticed lately more sirens squealing, more homes turned into smoky rubble playgrounds, more hushed conversations between grown ups with serious faces – his granny saying to his mother that she could not keep him in London any longer, it was selfish to have left it so late.

The little bus trundled up and down and round for what seemed like ages. Joe sat on his knees mesmerised by the endless fields. He had been transported into a wide open space a world away from the occasional tree and stamp of grass in London. When he squinted this looked like a huge bedspread made of green and yellow velvet; what he assumed were sheep, little white polka dots.

Pointed out from a distance the house was a tiny bed bug nestled in the folds of the giant bedspread, but when they got there it was actually was bigger inside than his own home. Home. Fleetingly he wondered what that meant now.

He shared a large room with another boy called Derek who spoke funny and was from a place called Brum. It was a nice room and Derek was all right. But at night he couldn't get used to the ink black sky, feeling it's weight, imagining it pushing through the window, past the flimsy curtains and smothering him. If this fear didn't wake him, the silence, startlingly interrupted by the strange animal noises, did.

But the little school felt familiar. The girls jumped with their ropes and made daisy chains. There was a football and a strange egg-shaped ball for the boys to throw and chase after across the mossy playing field. In his grey shorts and red tie, Joe fitted in. He made lots of friends and somehow made them laugh with what they called his funny, Cockney capers.

The food was good, collecting and picking it was fun and there was plenty of it. There was more space to run than he had ever experienced and his leg muscles stretched and filled out with the newly found freedom. The farm brought sounds and smells never imagined. The dog had puppies – by far the most disgusting and wonderful thing Joe had ever seen. Milking cows was disgusting too at first but the milk, if he managed to swig a bit before it went into the churn, was pure, warm, heaven.

At Christmas they pulled beside the fireplace the biggest tree Joe had ever seen indoors. Winter was hard. Joe had never felt the wind so fierce and cutting, but as the bedspread hills turned soft white he fixed his gaze, spread his arms like an eagle and screamed with delight as he and all his pals slid down them again and again until dusk crept in.

Lambs and daffodils, his sixth, seventh and eighth birthdays, new shoes, an even harsher winter, all came and went. Knowledge and his love of reading books stayed.

Throughout it all, every week, a piece of Joe's heart was pulled two hundred miles when a little envelope or postcard arrived bearing the beautiful, curly scribes from her fountain pen. News that his father was well, pictures of Big Ben, red buses, the guards at the palace – things now he wasn't sure he'd ever seen in real life – a regular reminder of home. He was missed so clearly. Loved so very dearly. He learned to write back and composed replies to the mother who became ever harder to imagine as a real living person.

There was talk at school – talk from grown-ups, reinvented, re-told for the playground, of destroyers, tanks, bombers and the Allied Forces, but what Joe didn't know was that his climb that Friday over the creaking stile, his rub of the sheepdog's head as he passed, the bread and dripping for his after school snack would be his last.

He wanted to return to London, longed for it some days, but he had become attached, connected in a real way to this place, nestled in the hills, to the simple life, to his refuge.

Just as he had so long ago, Joe stepped off the train and held the package close to his side. As the train pulled away Joe clutched his string-tied package to his chest and smelt the familiar smell of the sheepdog, the warm milk, the little bed bug farm that had been his escape, his shelter, his home. He heard the funny, alien, London accents, felt the hustle and bustle of the big city and then, down the platform he thought he saw her – smaller than he remembered.

'My mother?' he whispered.

The Girl and the Boy on the Train

May 1939

Ida stepped onto the train and held the suitcase close to her side. She walked through the connecting corridors of the train until an empty compartment was in sight. The jammed window trapped the heat and damp into the contained area so when other passengers opened the door, they turned around after one sniff or a muttered complaint. Ida would have sat in a truck full of livestock if it meant avoiding people.

'Papers please!'

The shout came through the carriages and Ida, scrambled to locate hers, dropping them with fumbling fingers, thankful that no one had witnessed her panic.

The inspector came in and held out his hand. These checks were becoming more frequent but at least this wasn't an SS man; the inspector wasn't even wearing the Party badge. He was stout with a twisted moustache that hid his lips, filtering the stench of tobacco and whiskey. The compartment door opened and a boy slipped in.

He wore the brown shirt that sent shivers down her spine. He was pale and thin, with dark blonde dishevelled hair. His face was chiselled into the structure of the idealised German, features Ida also shared. Along with her blonde hair teased into curls with old rags, and her blue eyes, this had proved a life-saver – making it easier to be Anna now and not Ida.

The boy started rummaging through his pockets. He took out a piece of paper which the inspector glanced at before leaving the cabin. The boy put a single brown leather case on the luggage rack and sat down facing her.

She watched his shoulders slacken and the colour return to his cheeks as his body sunk into the seat.

She tried to look casual; after all the suitcase by her feet created a superficial barrier between them, and if needed, a possible weapon. If anything happened, she could strike him with it, give herself time to run. He gazed out of the window, his expression unreadable. She pretended to do the same, but shot surreptitious glances in his direction.

The train rocked them gently across the countryside towards Hamburg. When it rolled into the next station, a succession of brown shirts ran past the window. The train screeched to a standstill.

Ida tried to stop her hands trembling as the trampling of the heavy boots and the shouts and screams from the other compartments got closer. She stole a look; his eyes were wide with fear, and for a split second, a mutual terror passed between them.

He leaned across suddenly and grabbed her, pulling her across the compartment. Silently, she squirmed and kicked out.

'Shhh, or this will be worse for you,' the boy said. His face brushed against hers, until his lips almost touched her skin. His breath was warm coffee. 'What is your name?'

'Anna Gerber.'

'Alfons Brandt. Get on my knee. It might save us both.'

She didn't answer.

'Please, they are nearly here.' His voice was softer and so was his touch as she obeyed.

They entered the carriage, two of them, smart in their uniforms, faces sneering.

'Gentlemen, a little privacy for me and my girl.' Alfons' voice had taken on a jovial tone but his hand was sticky with sweat against hers.

The uniforms hesitated.

'Comrades, we never get an empty carriage,' Alfons said.

'Papers!' The taller one stepped closer. He smoothed down his dark hair and fixed his attention on her. The other one lingered behind, shifting his weight from one foot to another.

Ida's papers should have stood up to close inspection. But it would be too dangerous if she was hauled into Gestapo headquarters. She shifted the material away from her dress carefully to reveal more of her legs and breasts as she took out her papers. Their eyes turned to her body.

Alfons dug his hand into his pockets and held his Hitler Youth membership up. The tall brown shirt frowned as he took the papers. The smile started to crack as Ida's papers were being scrutinised, but then shouts started in the next carriage. The uniforms threw the papers back at them and stomped out.

Out of the window, a man and woman were being dragged and kicked along the tracks. The train started up again, leaving Büchen station and the poor victims behind in a cloud of steam.

Ida moved away into her own seat. The train picked up speed.

'We live another day,' the boy said. He had a low voice, almost smoky, which moved through the carriage slowly.

'Do you have a death wish having no identity papers?' she hissed.

'You know some days I think I do, but apparently when it comes down to it, I don't.' He looked at her carefully again. 'You could have said you didn't know me. But I think you know what they would have done to me – as well as you.'

Her stomach flipped. 'What makes you think I don't have valid papers?'

'I saw your hands trembling,' he replied.

Despite all the months of practice, her body had betrayed her.

'You shouldn't worry,' he said. 'You look like a perfect little Bund Deutscher Mädel girl. Where are you off to – a hike, a climb or a lesson on becoming a wife, a mother, a homemaker?' There was a smile on his face but she wasn't sure whether to trust it.

'Heard camping is banned though,' he continued, 'after, what was it, nearly a thousand girls came back from Nürnberg with the beginnings of an army for *our Fuhrer* inside their bellies?'

She smiled then despite herself. He said *our Fuhrer* with a certain inflection that indicated hatred. This could just be a trick, yet even joking about something like that was dangerous. But how had he managed to get the Hitler Youth uniform? They were almost impossible to steal.

'I've never camped,' she replied and then blushed realising it sounded like she was referring to something else which she hadn't done yet either.

He raised an eyebrow. 'Is that right?' He lowered his voice. 'My neighbour Ursula was a BDM girl.'

Ida found herself inexplicably annoyed that he had mentioned a girl. But it pleased her. After all that had happened, she was still capable of frivolous emotion. In some ways she was still a normal seventeen year old.

'What happened to her?'

'She's still a BDM girl, a very devoted one,' he said 'devoted' with such bitterness that it changed the soothing rhythm of his voice. 'But let us not talk about bad people and bad things.' He stood and moved his leather satchel from the shelf and retrieved a small object. It was a bar of milk chocolate. He broke a piece off.

'Here,' he said, leaning across. Their fingertips brushed. She popped a small section in her mouth and swallowed without really tasting it. He looked up at her, his clear blue eyes right on hers. She reddened.

'So *Anna*—'

'So *Alfons*,' she cut in with equal sarcasm.

'What should we discuss? The meaning of life?'

'Most people who have the answers to that have been taken away,' she said. He raised his eyebrows and for a moment she thought this could be a trap after all.

'Are you going to eat the rest of that?'

She followed his gaze to the remaining chocolate which was starting to melt in her palm and stuffed it into her mouth in one go, almost choking herself in the process. This time she appreciated some of the flavour, a forgotten pleasure.

'Maybe you are not such a good BDM girl after all.' He laughed. It was a nice sound, and if she hadn't been grappling to establish a ladylike pose again, then she would have laughed too.

'Sorry.'

'Don't be sorry, you looked happy,' he said, 'even if you did nearly kill yourself eating it. Never be sorry for happiness.' He was fidgeting in his seat, eyes darting to the door and the window. 'We *could* pretend to be a couple.'

'What?'

'To pass the journey. To stop us thinking. It would be fun, like living again, properly, I mean.'

There was such sadness in his voice that she looked away from him. Fun belonged to before, when she was living rather than surviving each day. Ida had a lot of time to think about death because it was always following her. She felt like she understood it. Life was something she couldn't quite grasp. It seemed like so much effort and caused her constant worry and anguish.

Every day had been a battle since the night she'd watched those books burn when the Nazis first came into power. Even at the age of eleven, she'd understood that this was only the start of all of the trouble. Gradually life stopped being about living, about enjoying yourself, making friends, being yourself, going where you wanted to eat or drink and laugh, as it was for other teenagers. Ida had become so many things that she'd never realised she was or wanted to be; a half person or a 'mischling' as they like to call her.

'What does a normal couple in Germany talk about?' she asked, wanting a way out from all these thoughts, however temporary this would be.

'You like art?'

'I like sport,' she replied.

'You run?' he asked carefully.

'Yes.'

'How long have you been into this *running*?'

'Since the night of the broken glass.'

Her double life had started that cold November evening when the mobs came, burning the businesses and synagogues, smashing and beating their way through Berlin. Shards of windows littered the pavements, fire lit the sky and Ida left her life.

'Me too.'

'How do you… not give up when you feel… tired? How do you – ' Her voice broke on the last word. He looked at her in such a way that she knew he understood everything, about leaving people, losing people, never really getting to know people, living in anonymity.

'Easy, never look back.' He was trying to sound casual yet his face turned so pale it was almost marble. 'Even when you really want to.'

Tears started to prick at her eyes. She pressed her fingers against them.

'We are making each other sad,' he said gently. Then he leaned across the carriage again and whispered, 'You want to hear a joke?'

She nodded.

'You'll have to come here,' he said, patting the seat next to him. 'I don't want to say it too loud.'

She moved across cautiously. They were so close again, she could smell the worn-in scent of his uniform.

'Hitler visits a lunatic asylum. The patients give the Hitler salute. As he passes down the line he comes across a man who isn't saluting. "Why aren't you saluting like the others?" Hitler barks. "Mein Führer, I'm the nurse," comes the answer. "I'm not crazy!" '

She laughed but his eyes had a hard, far-away stare.

'Are you all right?' she asked.

He nodded, shifting in his seat and she caught a glimpse of skin through a tear in his shirt: abnormally smooth and pink in colour, raised up over the rest of his arm.

'Old wound,' he said, rubbing it briskly. He took the case from the rack and took out a small sewing kit, taking off his shirt to reveal a lean, muscular body.

'Do you have a rest from running soon? Maybe you will give it up?' he asked while expertly looping the thread through his battered uniform, securing it back into place. His voice started and ended, almost in rhythm with the needle as it went in and out repairing the cloth.

'Yes, very soon.'

'Me too.'

'You're good at that,' she remarked, watching him at work. 'My mother always said I had no patience for sewing.'

Her Mutta.

She had lost so many people by becoming Anna. Most of them still lived the same existence in her old neighbourhood; getting bread from old Fraulein Herbert's bakery at the end of the lane, going ice-skating, to the cinema or walking in the park. Those like her, who had changed their names, it was better not to know their lives. Those who stayed visible and waited to see what would happen, who barely left their houses, were slowly disappearing into an uncertain shadow. She couldn't even visit her mother's grave in case any of these people betrayed her.

'Nearly there,' Alfons said. Out of the window rich metal lines fell over themselves to form the archways of Hamburg station.

As they left the train, her heart thudded at the sight of all the people; the uniforms, the informers, the hidden trouble-makers who wanted to make money by finding the vanished. Perhaps there were some like her, whose insides were jittering so much that they never really stopped.

As he let go of her hand, she looked at his face and saw the same alertness under its surface. It was so strong that she could almost reach out and touch the fear. She hoped his path would be safe. It was unlikely they would meet again.

She turned to him. 'It has been –' He cut her off with an embrace that warmed her whole body. She hadn't been hugged in so long that she buried her face in his mended sleeve and bit her lip so that she wouldn't cry.

'My name is Kurt,' he whispered into her ear.

'I am Ida.' It felt nice to say her real name.

He stepped back and gave her one last smile. She would keep that with her good thoughts.

'Goodbye Ida, I wish you the best of luck,' he said quietly and walked away. He didn't look back.

Side by side

On April 25th 1915 Sheffield United beat Chelsea by three goals to nil in the FA Cup final at Old Trafford, the only Cup Final to be played in time of war...

Joe stepped off the train and held the package close to his side.

'What's up wi' thi Joe?'

'Nowt, I were just thinking about our Stan – seems funny 'im not bein' 'ere. 'e never missed a match.'

He put the bundle of brown paper in the pocket of his greatcoat.

'I'm sure 'e'd rather be out with the British Expeditionary Force bashin' the Hun.'

'Come on you two – we're gaggin' – let's go an' celebrate – shall we get half way back first?'

'Nah, let's get one at the Queen's Head, then come back and see the boys home eh? If we're late we'll sneak back through the hole in the wall.'

Joe sat with his pint, only half listening to his pals recounting the highlights of the game.

'I don't care what we paid for Utley – he were magnificent – a bloody rock at the heart of the team – him and Beau – if we could put up a battalion of men like them they'd have the Union Jack flying over Berlin by Easter. Two thousand pound! A bloody bargain!'

He might not have his brother with him but he was in good company here: men he would be proud to stand side by side with. Harry, who grew up in the next street, who he played with on the Rec as a kid and who signed up with him at the Corn Exchange back in September. Big Bob, the teacher from Healey who, at five foot five, had had to gain another inch in height through pride and another two around the chest in order to pass the medical. Chalkie, the Town Hall clerk, and Walter, the professor, who was smarter than the rest of them put together but who was as coarse as a miner after a pint or two.

They had been together for seven months now. That first day at the Drill Hall they were a shambles: a disparate bunch of individuals in an assortment of Norfolk Jackets, waistcoats, flat caps and Sunday best. They got their orders from the local papers, and it felt right that his first day's drill – six hours in the sun – was on the pitch at Bramall Lane, overlooked by those building the new Shoreham Street Kop. They practised rushing at Germans with brooms through the flower beds of Norfolk Park and they dug trenches on the lawns. There was a shortage of uniforms so their first ones, in bluey grey, made them look like convicts – or postmen. They moved from brooms to obsolete rifles. Now they were a proper disciplined unit, sat in proper khaki uniforms, and would soon be getting Lee Enfields – his brother could fire at least sixteen shots a minute with his.

They had headed up to the new barracks up on the moors at Redmires in December. Up there the new regimental Union Jack was torn to shreds by the weather within months, and they would wake up trapped in their huts by the drifting snow – it was then that Big Bob came into his own and was passed out through the window to get the door open.

Those route marches across Stanage in full battle order didn't half make men of them – if they didn't get pneumonia. It had been the best time of his life: having such good comrades, getting up at midnight at New Year to sing Auld Lang Syne outside the huts, the concerts at the YMCA hut, sneaking off to the Three Merry Lads and back through the hole in the wall, and the crowning moment: beating the Sherwood Forresters six goals to nil last Thursday! The colonel was strict but fair, and let them take leave for important things: like cup games at Bramall Lane – and today's trip to Manchester.

'What about Jimmy Simmons though? The way he crashed in Utley's centre! I bet his uncle were a proud man today. God bless the big man.'

'Aye, an' did tha see ol' Nudge there today an' all – done up in his best suit? Best captain United'll ever 'ave.'

Chalkie raised his glass: 'To Ernest 'Nudger' Needham and William 'Fatty' Foulke!'

'First goal I ever saw was scored by Needham,' Joe said. 'Replay of the third round of the cup against Newcastle, the last time we won it. I were only six, an' me an' our Stan got passed over people's head right to the front. I was scared stiff without my dad in that big crowd, but Stan looked after me.'

Stan was probably asleep in his bunk somewhere now; God, please let that be so; he would have gone to bed wondering what the score was – unless it got telegraphed to the front. Whatever he'd been doing today, he'd have been thinking about the United, checking his watch – kicking off now – willing the ball in Chelsea's net – half-time – final whistle.

He took the package out of his pocket – two programmes from the Cup Final and a "Sports Special" *Green 'un*. He'd wrapped them in the brown paper he'd got from the pie shop before the game to keep them from the weather. One programme for his old dad and one to send to Stan.

He regularly sent Stan match reports and cuttings from *The Independent*. Some snobs had wanted football cancelled at the outbreak of the war. But Stan said it gave them heart to read about their teams. It reminded them what they were fighting for. Those values that football embodied: sportsmanship, bravery, and working together for the greater good. And what about those who were flogging their guts out all week to raise coal or cast steel – doing their bit to stand up to the Kaiser – what else were they supposed to do with their leisure time? The one small escape each week from all the worry. Those Oxford and Cambridge men just didn't like people being paid to play sport – they didn't get football, the working man's game – didn't understand the fight with "sorrow for the young man's soul." Those same chin-less southerners didn't bark on about the cancellation of horse racing. Or opera, or golf, or West End theatre! "Business as usual" was a one-sided mantra. No, it was the poor who had to go and fight or sweat in foundries and have no pleasure, never smile, never cheer, until the war was won. Well, when it was all over, the ordinary folk, in return for winning the day, would demand their say in building the peace!

'Tha looks glum again Joe. I'll get thi another.'

'No, hadn't we best go back over to the station? Don't want to miss the boys' return.'

No one seemed to know what time the train was due in, but a crowd was building at the station, those in khaki, like them, getting pats on the back. There had been a lot of men in khaki at Old Trafford that afternoon, perhaps half the crowd. Some like themselves still in training, some on leave, others with bandages or walking on crutches. How his chest had swelled when fifty thousand voices sang 'God Save the King' before the teams walked out. He imagined the Kaiser hearing those voices and quaking. The sky was khaki too, especially in the second half: it was during half-time that the fog fell, yellowish and thick, as the band played 'Tipperary' and the crowd sang along. The only way you could tell there were people on the other side of the ground was from matches being struck or the glow of cigarettes or pipes. The light improved a little towards the end – the United with their long passing and rapier-like thrusts pushed aside the Beanstalk Club and their delicate passing play: over-powered them – just what they would do to Kaiser Bill. At the third goal, over-excited kids burst onto the field wanting to shake Joe Kitchen's hand.

Excitement started to build at Midland Station at around ten o'clock – the rumour was that the train was due in. They would miss the last tram up to Nether Green now, which meant an even longer walk up to Redmires – though a happy one. There must be over a thousand waiting. Then the train is heard pulling in and the cheering starts and chants of "Hi, Hi for the rowdy dowdy boys."

He only saw the heads of some of the players through the crowd – there was to be no triumphalism, no parading of the cup, they were just bundled into taxis and away into the night.

So that was it then. Another season over. No one believed that football could continue as normal through the next one: it would have to bend to the pressure. No Cup Final next year. Soon their battalion would be leaving the city to go and do their bit. Some had worried that all their training would be for nothing: that the Germans would cave in before last Christmas. That was not to be –

maybe next Christmas – then he and Stan could stand side by side on the terraces once more.

Wait

Joe stepped off the train and held the package close to his side. Suzy could see he was much thinner but her immediate response was that he looked so handsome, dashing even and she was surprised. The trademark Pearson family, unruly, black hair now sheared and slicked. The uniform made him look a proper man, distinguished. The slight limp the only indication of a story to be told.

He caught her eye and smiled. Her own smile faltered fleetingly with painful recognition. Joe, her fiancé's baby brother, now every inch a man and looking unnervingly similar to his sibling.

Joe greeted her with a cheeky grin. 'Hello sis.'

'I'm not your sister, Joseph Pearson!' Suzy said slapping his arm but immediately worrying in case he might have been injured there. She then tempered her automatic response with a quieter: 'Well, not yet anyway.'

They stood on the platform staring at each other.

'So…?' Joe eventually questioned, breaking the spell.

'Oh, yes, oh, well, erm, we've got you a room ready at ours, you've got what was Jean's room. It's still a bit flowery but we've just not been able to… to, you know, redecorate, because, you know, it's… there's…'

Joe smirked and let Suzy squirm before coming to her rescue: 'Because there's a war on? Yeah, so I heard.'

Suzy laughed. 'Shall I carry something ?' she asked, thinking about the walk ahead.

He scowled. 'Jerry might have cut short my war but I've not turned into a little girl you know. I can carry my own flamin' stuff.' Joe marched on ahead. Despite the limp he was fast. Suzy took the opportunity to scrutinise him from behind. The limp was slight and everything else looked fine. She wondered with a shudder if it was what you couldn't see that had rendered him unfit. Joe strode on unaware of her gaze, shoulders back, his sleek hair glistening in the sun.

With a little run, Suzy caught up and they eased into a chat. She gave him an up-date on the local news, comings, goings, departures and arrivals over the last year or so. She struggled to find anything to say that was cheerful without sounding utterly trivial. The reality was that things were hard. They had suffered terrible raids since August and there was no relenting. So many people were grieving and everyone else worrying. Although the days were busy and everyone tried to keep cheerful, at night the dark let the fear and the loneliness seep in.

As Suzy began to run out of news, the inevitable question came: 'So, when did you last hear from our Rob?' Joe's face turned anxious.

'Six weeks. I mean, he last wrote six weeks ago, so it's been a while really.'

'I bet he's writing and writing and they're getting all piled up somewhere.'

'That's happened before, I got four all at the same time in the summer.'

'Did he say where they were heading for?' Joe asked.

She shook her head. They both knew wherever it was, it wasn't somewhere nice. Joe nodded and they walked the last hundred yards in silent thought.

'Joseph Pearson! My God, it's good to see you lad.' Suzy's mother's arms clamped around Joe's back, squeezed the breath out of him then stood back staring, 'It's good to see you lad. It's good to see you,' she repeated, shaking her head at the skinny boy returned a handsome man. 'Come on, come on in. There's tea and some bread and butter waiting for you, come on in.

'Thank you, Mrs Johnson.'

'If you're to stay here you can't be calling me that. It's Maggie.'

'Thank you, Maggie. I've got something for you.'

Joe unwrapped his brown paper packet.

'On my way back from Louvain through Belgium I got a one of the Flemish nurses to get me something.' He brought a piece of lace out of the paper.

'It's for on a tray or dressing table or something. Handmade. And this is for you Suzy.' He handed her something wrapped in tissue paper. 'It's a thing you can sew onto a dress apparently. She kept saying it was for Bertha. But I said no, it's for Suzy.'

Suzy took out the delicate lace collar.

'It's beautiful. You shouldn't have.'

'Well, I figured Rob can't be here, but I can. He would have bought you something, and he's my flesh and blood, so it's as good as him giving it you.'

Mrs Johnson held up the dainty lacework. 'So delicate, so much work!' She planted a kiss on his cheek and made him blush.

'We've got what was our Jean's room ready for you. It's still a bit flowery but we've just not been able to...' Mrs Johnson stopped mid-sentence in puzzlement as Suzy and Joe looked at each other and started to laugh.

For a number of years now it had just been Suzy and her mother. Her courting with Rob had been very short and he had asked her to marry him when he knew he was leaving so they'd not had much time together as a couple. It was strange having Joe there, having a man about the house. There were a few awkward moments – trying to pass on the narrow stairs, both coming out of their rooms onto the little landing at the same time – that lead Suzy to start paying attention to his whereabouts in the house. She kept catching herself staring at him just moving, bending to strike a match on the grate, hauling a bag of potatoes with ease. He used to be scrawny, a lanky lad and although he did look thin he seemed wider, more complete. Four years in the army – one of those with the BEF in Belgium – and a lifetime of experiences had changed him. He wasn't a child any more.

Joe wasn't short of things to do with his days. With very few men left behind in the town, he soon had a list of things to be getting on with, working with old Eddie fixing tiles back on to the post office roof, hauling sand bags up against the wall of the bank, making a new gate for the school, or helping salvage belongings from bomb damaged homes. At the end of the day he'd come back to the house. Suzy or her mother would cook and they would eat together, talking about their days. Joe made her cry with laughter with his different accents imitating the people he'd met while he'd been away – the officer with the stammer who couldn't quite get his orders out in time, the hot-headed Geordie who wanted to fight everyone, no matter what side they were on. Suzy quieted though when there was talk of Missy, the nurse who'd played backgammon with him when he couldn't sleep at night. But he said nothing of the war itself, as if he didn't want it to intrude into their house. No mention of the explosion from which he had to be dragged to survival – shattering his leg and sending him home.

The war, though, had a nasty way of making its

presence known. For weeks on end through November bombs fell nearly every night somewhere over the city. Families either huddled into their own draughty, dripping shelters or crammed in with the masses under the concrete for hours on end. The singing couldn't drown out the sounds. Joe paced around or held Suzy's hand to stop it shaking.

After a few such nights he could no longer stand his feelings of helplessness and signed up for the ARP to take up fire-watching.

'I'd rather be outdoing something useful, than lurking like a coward,' he said.

Suzy wanted to plead with him not to do it. He had done his bit. Suffered enough. She wanted, needed, to keep him safe. But after tea he'd head straight back out in his uniform, tin helmet on his head.

The new year brought the first real nips of winter cold, snow and yet more bombs. Joe returned after long nights, sooted and weary.

Weeks passed. The bombs stopped falling. The Americans joined the war and the nation felt it no longer stood alone. A letter arrived from Rob. His infantry division was being sent from Arabia to the Far East.

Suzy didn't want to tempt fate and give voice to her fears, but she confided in Joe: 'I'm really worried for him. The news from Singapore has been frightful.'

'You know he couldn't have lived with himself if he'd stayed. You mustn't worry about our Rob. He's a survivor. Just you see. It's those Japs you should worry for when he gets stuck into them. When we got into scrapes as kids he'd always come up smiling and smelling of roses. It was me that got into bother, not him.'

Spring turned into a glorious summer. Suzy was busy
with the children at school; Joe was more than occupied
with the town's repairs and maintenance. But the long,
drawn out evenings, fading into a mellow warmth, took
them walking along the canal towpaths and into another
world. Suzy picked flowers; Joe skimmed stones on the
flat water. Neither they nor dragonflies gliding lazily
around them, appearing to have much to worry about.

One evening when Joe had gone upstairs to get ready
to go out to the pub, Suzy went to her room to get her
book so that she could curl up for the evening by the
fireside. A movement caught her eye through a narrow gap
in the door to Joe's room. He was standing at the
washstand with his shirt off, squeezing a flannel in the
bowl. His pale white torso was patterned with criss-crosses
of scars, like scattered flowers, the flesh uneven, as if bites
had been taken from the muscles of his chest and
shoulder. She stood guiltily transfixed – his body and
movements strangely beautiful.

The post the next morning brought strange words all
the way from Burma: "missing presumed dead."

The following winter was one of the cruellest in
memory. Temperatures fell twenty or more below
freezing, the skies were heavy and grey and brought snow.

Come spring, the blanket of melancholy that had
settled over Joe, over the house, seemed to fall away.
There was no more news about Rob and the rhythm of
their daily life continued, Suzy enjoying the lighter nights.
Strolling again, by the canal, with Joe.

It was towards the end of July of 1942. Joe had gone into Birmingham for the evening with some of his friends. Suzy and her mother were about to turn in when the siren's wail struck up.

'Surely not?' said her mother.

'We should still go mother. Come on, get your coat on. It's probably nothing but best be safe.'

'I shall finish my Ovaltine first. Bloody Hitler!'

'Mother!'

Not everyone was heading down the street with them. Some defiantly stuck two fingers up and stayed put. The shelter was full nonetheless when the first distant rumbles started. They felt the ground shake as the booms got nearer.

Suzy prayed that Joe was safe somewhere.

'I don't like it in here, I don't like that noise,' whispered a tiny voice as another boom drowned out the singing and sent a shock of tension through the huddle. A little head buried itself into Suzy's skirt. With several children gathered around her, Suzy told all the stories she could think of in as light a voice as she could muster as the booms and thumps echoed around them. Miraculously, one by one the children fell asleep.

The bombardment went on and on.

'There'll be nothing left of Birmingham by morning.'

'It's just a sign Hitler's losing it. This is revenge for the pounding he's taking. It's the last throws of a desperate man, you see,' a voice in the dark tried to reassure.

People tried to sleep, but it was with bleary eyes that they emerged to the all-clear, blinking into the early morning light. Suzy felt numb, paralysed with the hours of fear, her imagination of what might have happened to Joe all too vivid. With the children reassured and safely dispatched home, Suzy took her mother's arm, neither of them daring to speak as they approached their street for fear of what they might find.

All across the city was a pall of smoke, but their street was untouched. Suzy got her mother sat down at a neighbour's with a cup of tea before heading back out into the street to start a search she didn't know how to begin to face. But then, walking towards her with the slight limp, Joe was coming, alive and well; grave concern and then momentous relief flooding his face as he saw her. Suzy ran. The power of thought had drained away and instinct took over. She leapt into Joe's arms, wrapping her legs around him.

'My God, my God, thank God.' Joe said over and over again as he buried his face in her neck. Suzy sobbed on his shoulder as he held her. Neither of them knew how long they had stayed like that before Joe lowered Suzy to her feet, took her face in his hands and kissed her.

The war ground on, but no more bombs fell and it felt like a corner was turned; the first buds of hope began to push through. The routine of their productive days and companionable evenings continued but something fundamental had shifted. Suzy's silent journey across the little landing to Joe's room became a nightly event. She ran her fingers over the flowers on his chest. Sometimes Joe talked in his sleep as she lay by his side. Sometimes he cried out, lashed out an invisible foe. Suzy stroked his forehead and shushed him back to sleep; watching his peaceful slumber, all that she ever wanted.

By the time that the Allies marched on Paris a wedding was hastily arranged with a beautiful cardboard cake for the photographs. Suzy felt terrible guilt that it was the "wrong" brother that gave her his vow, even if it felt so right. But the reality was Rob was dead; she had to do the right thing for the living, for the love she felt and for the life inside her. Afterwards they went down by the canal where they sat in the late summer sunshine, full from the picnic and blackberries, and Suzy giggled as Joe gently rubbed the bump and told his baby, in his funny accents, about all the good things life was going to bring when the war ended. Suzy listened to the promises of better times, a little house with a garden and a cupboard full of pudding. She smiled and sighed contentedly, knowing that in the man she loved so completely she already had all she would ever really need.

Their first wedding anniversary was a double celebration: the war, that at one time felt like it would never end was finally over with the surrender of the Japanese. They took little Joseph for a picnic in the park and watched him take his first steps across the grass. As early evening drew in, they pulled themselves reluctantly from their perfect afternoon and strolled lazily, hand in hand back to the house, little Joe riding on big Joe's shoulders. They chatted and giggled easily with a life that was growing ever more optimistic. Joe planted a kiss on Suzy's cheek as he reached to lovingly tease a stray daisy from her hair.

'Mother we're back.' She opened the door and froze.

He looked gaunt, his cheekbones prominent, his eyes sunken, but still handsome, the trademark Pearson family, unruly, black hair sheared and slicked.

'Hello Suzy,' Rob said.

Pavilion

Indian soldiers serving under British command in India, formed one-fifth of the British Army. Over a million of these 'sepoys,' fought in the Great War and over 70,000 died

Jaspreet stepped off the train and held the package close to his chest. He brushed the coal and steam smell off his hair and breathed in the salty sea air of Brighton. The walk to the Indian Hospital would clear his head and shake off his worry about visiting his friend. He walked along the road, the sea spray almost palpable and the moisture-laden air with the cries of sea gulls, lending a strange background noise, so different from the gloom-ridden streets of London he had left that morning. He ambled along, slowly. He straightened his shoulders, held that package tightly and hoped that this visit would not be the last.

It was kind of colonel sahib of the 47th Sikh Regiment to inform him of Gurbachan's survival and recuperation in the Pavilion hospital. They were the sixty eight men out of the two hundred and eighty who had survived the German bombing at La Bassée. There was even mention in the British Parliament of their bravery for destroying that German base.

Jaspreet shook his head. At what cost? How many had died in this dreadful battle? None of them had any idea of the battle conditions when they had enrolled. The snow, the German bombs, the mud and cold that seeped through their tropical bodies had to be experienced. He remembered scrambling on the mired earth, limbs torn in places by the barbed wire, the stench of dead bodies that could not be moved out of the trenches immediately. He was lucky, one of the few who had escaped with few wounds that healed quickly and he had a few months off recuperating at a Sikh friend's house in London. He shuddered, thinking of the others and turned his face up to the vague sun that played hide and seek in the sky. He wanted the warmth of the Punjab, his poor farm and his family. Then his thoughts turned to Gurbachan. He should think of him and stop wallowing in this self-pity.

The Indian Hospital almost took his breath away. It was far from what he expected. It really was a palace, surrounded by beautiful gardens: such a strange mixture of Indian and British design. He looked up at the domes and minarets, such a different architecture to anything he had seen in this grey land. He felt a tiny bit of pride that here was a bit of India in this faraway country. Pride that his comrades were afforded such accommodation. The guard at the gate questioned him, read his letter from the hospital and allowed him in after quite a long wait. He walked into the amazing building, keenly observing each and every bit of this marvellous palace. The nurse, who opened the door to a huge hall, took the slip from his hand and indicated that he follow her. The room was vast! He had never seen such a big space in his life. The ornate lotus shaped chandeliers with gilt-edged dragons hung from the ceiling like exotic birds of paradise, casting a luxurious, decadent look in a place of pain and suffering. There were rows and rows of beds as far as his eyes could see. Turbaned Sikh men, wounded and bandaged, were in the beds, a *sepoy*, nurse or auxiliary standing beside some of them.

Jaspreet tried to take it all in and felt light-headed.

"Nearly seven hundred beds," said the nurse as she

walked him down the long room. Several curious eyes followed him and he looked for the familiar face of Gurbachan.

He lay there, torso in bandage, legs absent, his arms in bandage, almost like a mummy. A frightened face peeked out of the turban that again covered a bandage. It was as bad as Jaspreet had imagined. He felt a sharp pain that seared through him as if one of the German bombs had ripped through his rib cage. He managed a smile and put the package down on the bed and said a faint *"Sasrikal"* to Gurbachan, tears welling up in his eyes, controlling them, holding his head high and willing them not to roll down his cheeks.

That package with the little bits of India that he could collect, stayed intact. It contained a small *Guru Granth Sahib*, the prayer book, a small piece of that Indian sweet that his land lady had given him, a sweet made with rationed sugar that she had made for the valiant, 'Kings of Punjab' as she called the soldiers, in awe of them ready to give up their lives for king and country. There was also a jar of pickles that she had prepared, pickles with the sharp pungent flavour of hot mango that he hoped Gurbachan could savour. Now he was not sure. That pathetic package, would it give him any comfort at all? His words stuck in his throat and he swallowed, any words he struggled to find going down with his saliva. A silence enveloped them.

Had his friend fainted? Should he call a nurse? Jaspreet panicked as he saw Gurbachan's eyes rolling upwards and closing. A laboured breathing was all he could hear. Should he run over to the nearest member of staff? He was hesitant, not knowing if he had caused the fainting.

Was Gurbachan shocked at seeing Jaspreet looking fit

and healthy? He felt guilty, unsure what to do.

Then he heard a rumbling noise of laughter and joy. Jaspreet turned around to find where it was coming from. A group of visiting men, looking rather splendid in their uniforms, approached, talking loudly to the other men in the beds and the staff in the hall. Jaspreet stood at the bedside, not raising his head till he heard footsteps beside him. The men were in a group near the bed next to Gurbachan's.

He saw her then, a striking, regal-looking woman in a Red Cross nurse's uniform. Her bearing was like one of the white memsahibs he had seen in London. Yet she had some Indian features. He was intrigued. She spoke in English and said something kind to the man in the next bed and then handed him a photo. An Indian nurse came and stood beside Jaspreet, tapping him on the shoulder. He shrank away, worried that he had done something wrong. She smiled and addressed him in Punjabi.

'That is Sophia memsahib, the daughter of Maharajah Duleep Singh. She comes and helps us.' Memsahib Sophia Duleep Singh: their very own royalty! Daughter of the Maharajah. She who walks through the palaces of the Empire, god-daughter to Queen Victoria herself. Bringing succour in a faraway land. A saint amongst mortals: who did so much to fight for her broken countrymen. Jaspreet stood and tried not to gawp. The nurse smiled, bustled past him, and tidied the bed. Then she woke Gurbachan. Jaspreet sighed in relief as his friend opened his eyes.

'Sophia memsahib,' whispered Gurbachan. As the princess neared his bed, his whole face lit up and a smile creased his lips. Jaspreet felt the strength seeping from his limbs as she approached.

She spoke to Gurbachan in a quiet tone, gave him a

photo, smoothed his bed cover and touched his face softly. Gurbachan seemed to get a new lease of life. His eyes sparkled and he tried to raise his arm. She gently put it down again.

'I'll come visit you again. I'm so proud of what you have done for this country,' she said and moved on to the next bed.

Gurbachan's eyes moved towards Jaspreet's. He lifted his bandaged arm and raised his eyebrows. He mouthed 'How are you?' The tears rolled down Jaspreet's cheeks. He sobbed silently, wiped his eyes and touched his friend's arm. The white cotton bandage was cool to his touch but his heart burned with a rage that made him sweat. He sat there watching his once bright, strong friend who could make the regiment laugh with his jokes and songs lying in a white heap of helplessness. A nurse approached them and in a kind voice asked how he was, administered some medicine and left after making him comfortable.

'That memsahib is the reason I'm alive. I'm being well looked after,' whispered Gurbachan. His smile was reassuring.

The shock of the first sighting of his friend faded away slowly. This grand palace, with its Gurdwara, this Indian princess moving amongst the English royalty. Their role in the great struggle would be remembered. This war would change so much – they were now respected. Equals in struggle, equals in adversity, equals in death. We who fought so hard, trampled in the mired earth, so that others could breathe the sweet air of freedom.

Jaspreet even managed to open the package and fed him a small piece of the sweet *mithai*. He asked if he wanted him to read a prayer from the book. Gurbachan nodded so Jaspreet read it softly and watched as his friend's eyes moistened. They felt close as if a calling to that higher being had given them both some comfort. Jaspreet closed his eyes and prayed for Gurbachan's quick recovery.

The Long Journey Home

Tommy Atkins could not wait to get on the train that would take him to Calais, then after that a short trip across the water back to his beloved England.

As the train came into the station he boarded with all the other men being permitted to return from the war. He put his rucksack down beside him and felt the motion of the train as it pulled out of the station.

Everyone said the war was only going to last a couple of weeks; but the weeks had turned into long months. Home sweet home! He could not wait to see his wife and give her that first kiss.

As he looked for a compartment he passed a man who had his vesta case out and was lighting up. The man ignored him and walked straight past. He'd half a mind to teach him some manners but one thing the war had taught him was that it takes all sorts. He found a space in a compartment chock-a-block with soldiers.

The last memories he had was going over the top and they had all surged forward into a seething mass of explosions and bullet fire. It was hard to make out anything at all.

But, soon he would be home. His whole family would be there for a good old Christmas dinner: his wife, mother and his darling boy, little Tommy. Except he would not be so little now. Ready for starting school. He was only a nipper when he'd left.

Last Christmas had been spent in the bunker sharing out army rations and Christmas presents. Then through the still air came the strains of Silent Night, and the British started to sing along. They had all abandoned their positions, and started to sing. Someone played a mouth organ. Slowly one German soldier put his hands up and came to the centre of the muddy field and one of our boys went out to meet him unarmed. In the middle of nowhere bit by bit all the troops came out to meet each other and shake hands and wish each other a merry Christmas. They brought out pictures of their girlfriends, wives, mothers and children. Then a football was found, and it was there in No Man's Land, some sort of God's simple love was found at Christmas time. They all had a laugh and a little bit of good cheer even if they did not really understand each other. After all it was the time of goodwill to all men.

But all too soon the festivities were over and they all had to return to the bunker, but they shook hands and some even kissed and hugged each other for the love of a baby in a manger. All men, on both sides, could understand that simple message of love.

The next day, everything went back to normal and the war continued.

The trained pulled into Calais. He lifted up his rucksack and followed the others to the gangway up to the ferry. He joined all the men standing in line. He took out his pack of cigarettes and asked a young lad if he would like one, but he either did not seem to see him or even hear him. Most likely shell shock.

Soon he was on board the boat with all the men returning home; some were in a worse state than others, some being carried on stretchers in a sorry condition with bandages on their heads and others had bandages over their eyes.

Some of the men played a game of cards as they crossed the channel. He contented himself looking at pictures of his family and dreaming about that lovely Christmas dinner his wife and mother will be preparing.

He could taste in his mouth that boiled brisket, those lovely roast potatoes, and mother's wonderful sherry trifle. His mouth watered at the thought of it.

It was an easier crossing, smooth, not rough like the one coming to France in 1914, and soon Dover's cliffs came into view: tall white and magnificent. Once again he managed to push his way through the crowd and get a seat next to a window on the train to London. It was so good to be safe and sound on British soil. He could not wait to have a nice hot bath and sleep in crisp, clean bed linen. He could not remember the last time he had done that! To make love again after such a long time and feel his wife's loving embrace, and be kissed. Warmth after all the coldness of war and the trenches. The safeness of her caresses and kisses. He smiled to himself at the thought of that long first kiss and the look on her face when he walked through the door.

London's streets were busy, just like they always were. He lit another cigarette as he waited for the bus to take him home to dear old Camden Town. He boarded in his turn; but the bus conductor just waved a finger at him and said next please. He must get free bus travel returning from the war. He sat by the window and drank in the sights of home.

He walked up his street, the street where he used to play as a nipper, the same street where he started his first home after he married. The door was ajar and all the lights were on, a fire blazing in the range. The party had already started without him. He stood on the threshold of the living room. He could see the whole family sat round the Christmas table with all the food waiting to be served. His seat was empty and the place was set waiting for him. It smelt and looked delicious. He wanted to surprise them.

He entered and sat down at his place, but everyone ignored him.

Then they all raised their glasses to a picture of him on the mantelshelf – in his army uniform.

It was his wife that spoke first:

"Here is to you Tommy boy. We will never forget you, or your sacrifice for King and Country. A wonderful husband. A loving father, and a dutiful son!'

'Aye, to Tommy! God bless him.'

He hung his head and wept dry silent tears.

Silence

Ellen stepped off the train and held the album close to her side. The photographs helped to focus her thoughts; stopped them drifting. Standing in the tide of commuters she looked about her at Lime Street Station. She saw nothing of what there was now. She remembered the sirens that sounded in 1940 – then she remembered the silence.

Silence was the moment before. The moment you waited, counting the seconds in your head. Silence was the moment when you stopped breathing – there was no fear, only resignation and acknowledgement. Silence lasted no longer than several heartbeats. Silence – and the leaves stirred on the great chestnut, a tree which had stood for a hundred years. Its petals threaded through the first green sprigs of growth and twisted down to the paving stones like moths, to lie flattened on the damp ground. The tree, in its season-set shades, caught in the irreverent storms and brindled by winters – had endured. There had been something comforting in that, especially in the silence.

Silence was the moment when the whistle of the falling bomb had ceased. This meant it would fall close, too close. If the whistling sound did not stop then the bomb would fall further: Wavertree or the Mistry. The bombers used to turn in from the river at the Liver Buildings, beating inland to empty their cargo. Silence was their moment. They made the silence. For some the sound of the engines throbbing would never go away. For others there was silence – forever.

At then end of the silence there was destruction. There was loss. The moments passed, fleeting as the blast had ricocheted off the buildings again and again as if the sound would never die. The windows were all blown in, frames and all and the leaves of the chestnut stirred. Time was the essence of silence. The city had been transfigured by the bombs and then by time. It was years since the lists of the dead were posted and now the names had been forgotten and eroded. But she had not forgotten, she had come back and she would remember them - until there was silence.

Ever Yours

Jo stepped off the train and held the package close to her side. Andy had given it to her at Lincoln station with strict instructions not to open it until she got home. She had turned it over in her hands and held it on her lap as the train had taken her away. And now, here she was, back at Victoria Station, back in Sheffield – this time without a return ticket. It felt a lifetime away; her life here – as it was back then. So much had changed.

John had enlisted in 1939 and left her with an empty house and another black eye. If only she had not lost his baby, perhaps things could have been different. He had been captured at Dunkirk and had spent his war in various POW camps. The telegram she received last week from her sister said he was on his way back, bringing back to her mind memories she had managed to bury these last few years. She went for days on end not even thinking about him, and what's more she no longer felt much guilt. Now it was unavoidable. She was nearly home – if you could call it that. Would being cooped up have changed him, or would there be years of pent up frustration?

After he had left, and the war progressed, she had found her life without meaning: keeping house for ghosts. So she had handed the keys of her house to her sister and signed up for the Womens' Land Army. It had been the best decision she had ever made.

The hostel she was sent to for her training was an old mansion house with a sweeping gravel drive, fringed with rhododendrons, leading up to the porticoed front door. The entrance hall with two oak staircases was big enough to fit the whole of her Heeley terrace inside. Paintings of severe-looking people hung on the walls and she was instructed to remove her boots so as not to damage the polished parquet floor.

The company of the two dozen other girls was a tonic, as was the routine: on the farm for seven in the morning, breakfast at eight, tea at six, and in bed by ten or they would have Matron to answer to. Jo's dormitory, which she shared with five others, was in the old drawing room, and they ate together in the splendour of the dining room with views over the lawns where pheasants strolled.

She took to the animals straightaway, the shorthorns yielding their milk to her like they had always known her; and cleaning the stalls gave her a sense of purpose. If the cows were sweet-natured and patient, the pigs were playful and full of individual character: pulling at her dungarees as she tried to clean their pens. She soon knew them all by name. She discovered the places where the hens tried to hide their eggs and learnt that the ones that floated when placed in a bowl of water had to be thrown away. They organised trips to the village church and attended ENSA shows, or dances at the village hall along with young men from the local RAF base – though after cutting hedges with bill hooks or clearing fields of nettles, thistles or dock, she could barely stand on her feet. She had never experienced such physical fatigue in her life – but it meant the camp bed and lumpy mattress were no barrier to sleep.

Then at harvest time it was flat out to cut the corn. First they used scythes to open up a headland from the gate to allow the beautiful Suffolk Punches in with the cutter and binder; then the girls set to stooking the sheaves. It was nothing like she had imagined from a painting she had once seen – languid and peaceful: this was hard, dirty, sweaty work. Then the stooks had to be turned to dry them, then taken by cart to the stack yard. In between this and milking and looking after pigs there were the hay fields to clear and pitch forks to be mastered – how hard it actually was to throw hay onto a cart without scattering it everywhere!

Those first few months were a whirl and she went from townie housewife to capable farmhand at a rate that astonished her. But, training over, the Manor Farm Gang were disbanded and the Land Army committee rep came to tell them where they were to be posted. A truck took them to the station and at the other end she was met by Mrs Snaith, the farmer's wife, in a van and driven to the farm in the Wolds that was to be her new home and place of work.

'We've already got one Land Girl at the farm, but we've work for another, now that Jack has gone off to serve his country.'

She was shown up a creaking staircase to an attic room with sloping ceilings, a double bed and views out over the fields leading down to a small copse. As she opened her small suitcase on the bed there was a knock at the door and a tall handsome girl strode in thrusting her hand out eagerly. She wore the WLA uniform of v-neck khaki sweater, green tie, knee breeches and knee-high socks.

'They said you'd arrived. How super! I'm Andrea, but you can call me Andy. Oh, I'm pleased to have some proper company. Been here five weeks now and, well, the Snaiths are jolly decent and all, but it's not the same is it. We've got to share a room I'm afraid, not exactly Land Army regulations but we'll manage won't we? It would be bad luck to use their Howard's room, what with him going off to fight: need to keep it the same, don't you think.

Which side of the bed do you prefer?'

Jo's face must have betrayed her feelings.

'Oh, I'm sorry, I always do that: talk too much and too fast and don't let anyone get a word in edgeways! It's nerves you know, runs in the family.'

She finally shut up and Jo introduced herself.

She would have to complain to the local rep about the accommodation and sleeping arrangements.

Andy gave her the tour of the farm and introduced her to all the animals.

'They let me ride Maisie and go out to the fields to bring the calves in. Do you ride? Oh you must! I'll teach you.'

It turned out that Andy had had her own horse when she was growing up in Hertfordshire and used to ride with the hunt.

After a less than comfortable night spent self-consciously on the foot's width of the bed nearest the wall, she was relieved to be woken at six by a cheery Mrs Snaith bringing two cups of tea.

They were straight out to the milking sheds where the fourteen year-old daughter was already hand milking. Then after breakfast they cleared out the sheds before joining the others in the orchard to pick the apple harvest. In the afternoon, whilst they were out in a field raking couch-grass, great grey clouds rolled in off the North Sea and unleashed their worst. They were thoroughly soaked and covered in mud by the time they had finished, but Andy had kept her spirits up with her chatter and her Marlene Dietrich impersonations, which had her in stitches:

'Outside the barracks, by the corner light, I'll always stand and wait for you at night. We will create a world for two, I'll wait for you, the whole night through, For you, Lili Marleen, For you, Lili Marleen.' Andy let her have the first use of the bath water when they got back.

They were given the occasional evening off. Mr Snaith went to visit his aunt in Louth and gave them a lift there and back. They went to the picture house where they saw *The Man in Grey*. It was towards the end of the film when James Mason attacks Margaret Lockwood that Jo started to cry. She tried to brush it off as nothing but that night in their room John's mistreatment of her came flooding out.

Andy was kind to her and grew on her day by day. Once she had seen past her loud and posh exterior she saw her for the unselfish and funny person she was: totally unaware of her own ungainliness and the ungraceful way she clomped around the farm in her gumboots. Andy turned out to be a demon with a pitchfork too.

The threshing machine arrived in the yard and a steam traction-engine trundled into position. They were set for an arduous couple of days threshing the corn and a stack of beans.

'Tuck those dungarees into your socks and grab a pitchfork,' Mr Snaith said, 'it's going to get lively.'

She soon found out what he meant. As they started to take down the first stack, rats and mice seemingly came from nowhere. Jo squealed, not because she was not used to seeing them around the farm, but they now moved unpredictably.

'Just think of them as Jerries,' shouted Andy as she started lunging and whacking.

Rather than take part in the sport, Jo preferred to feed the machine, cutting bands off the sheaves and getting covered in dust and chaff. They had to work flat out to keep up with the iron beast and to drag away the rapidly filling, heavy sacks of corn. Andy had the knack of swinging these onto her back and strode up the ladder to the loft of the barn, leaving Jo huffing and puffing to keep up, spitting out lungfuls of dust.

She never did put in that complaint about the accommodation to the local rep. In fact she got used to sharing a bed, found it a comfort, and even took to holding Andy's hand before drifting off to sleep.

Then one night as they were heading back from seeing to the pigs a great roar of planes filled the air, flying in close formation with all their lights blazing. They stood in awe, they were used to seeing squadrons of Lancasters coming and going but now one wave followed another. This was different. Andy cheered and waved and shrieked, then turned and hugged Jo, picked her off her feet and swirled her round.

'Don't you see what this means? They're off to finish Hitler at last. Go on boys! Go on!' she shouted.

Jo burst into tears. 'Oh Andy, does this mean it's coming to an end?'

'Oh I jolly well hope so, you funny, dear, old thing,' she said, putting her arm round Jo.

That night, wide awake, her head full of thoughts, Jo rested her head on Andy's shoulder. Andy stroked her hair.

From Victoria Station, Jo took the tram up into town. Peace had not yet been secured throughout the world but, since she was last here at Christmas, a dark, heavy weight had been lifted from the town and its citizens; grim determination in people's faces had been replaced by hope.

Her sister had left the house spotless – better than she herself had left it. John might be here as soon as tomorrow. There were daffodils in a vase on a Nottingham lace table cloth.

Jo sat at the table and started to open the package. There was a note and something wrapped in a silk handkerchief – a gold-coloured necklace with gaudy stones on it. She unfolded the note which was embossed with a Hertfordshire address. It read:

"Dearest Jo, this belonged to my grandmother. It is very valuable – so whatever you do, do not take it to a pawn shop. Get it properly valued first. Hide it somewhere, or, better still, take it to a bank. Then if ever you need to escape you will have the means.

Surely tomorrow, you'll feel blue
But then will come a love that's new

Ever yours,

Andy."

The Flight of a Falling Bomb

Many things can be flattened by high explosives, and social barriers are among them.

Mrs Driver thought herself a cut above. She had the end-of-terrace house but called it 'semi-detached'. When asked where she lived, she named the road at the side of her house, although the post on her front doormat shared our street name. Her husband was deputy office manager in the print-works' accounts department. He had an inky-cuff, indoors job with responsibility and two giggling girls under him. His extra couple of shillings a week let Mrs Driver pay for a charlady and on Friday mornings when the street donkey-stoned their steps, Mrs Driver stood like a duchess, looking down literally on the wobbling backside of her woman-that-does and metaphorically on the rest of the street.

However, there was something our house had that hers lacked, for all it's end-of-terrace splendour: we had a good, dry cellar. What's more, father had fitted it out as a bomb shelter during his last spell of leave. Some planks and four-by-two had, in the hands of a ship's carpenter (first class), become a comfortable bench and three bunk beds. As soon as the siren sounded, mum would send us downstairs with our blankets and pillows then open the front door so that Mrs Driver could join us. By the time we little ones, tottering under our candlewick and goose-feather burdens, had struggled to the hallway, we could hear Mrs Driver's heels clicking over the cobbles as she fast-waddled her way down the street.

During the raids, she sat with knuckles shining white in the dim light of the storm lantern as she clung to her patent-leather handbag. That bag never left her hands and we whispered between our bunks that it was stuffed with the greatest treasures of her dustless, childless, semi-detached palace – Arabian jewels and fivers made during clandestine night-shifts at the print-works. Mr Driver was left at home to protect the rest of her moveable wealth from the sticky fingers of urchins from the rough end of the street.

Mrs Driver perched on the bench, refusing mum's offers to get her head down on the empty bunk. Wouldn't dream of it. Couldn't put you to the trouble. I'll just sit here a while until the worst of it's over. In case the children take fright. In case you need help.

While we kids, wide-eyed and wakeful, listened to the distant crump of bombs and whispered excitedly about which of our teachers that last one had landed on (hope that was Mr Roberts – no geography tomorrow. That one was Mr Grant – no more press-ups and rugby. Hope that wasn't Miss Roberts with her kind words and biscuits) Mrs Driver sat there, sticky palmed and short-breathed, in case the children took fright.

The all-clear called Mrs Driver to her feet, her dignity returning as she shook her dress free of creases. That's that then. I'll be off. I'm sure the children will be fine now.

We'd follow her up the stairs and listen to her tread – more measured going than it was coming – as she strutted off to see if Mr Driver had kept the best china safe from ne'er-do-wells and long-range bombers.

There was another reason why Mrs Driver refused the offer of the bunk. It was meant for cousin Betty but it was empty because she was upstairs with a man. The stain of association would have kept Mrs Driver out of that bunk if the raid had lasted as long as Noah's flood.

Cousin Betty was often upstairs with a man. Air-raids put the town on the front line and there was no way for any of us to know if death would be knocking hard on the door before morning. Such immediate menace made threats of neighbourly disapproval and damaged reputations seem small and distant. Betty's first love hadn't got past Dunkirk and she wasn't going to go to her grave wondering about any of life's pleasures.

Mum didn't like it but, since Betty was father's niece, she didn't feel she could put her foot down. Besides, the girl was only with us because Dad's widowed sister had been taken by a five-hundred-pounder. When the veil between life and death was so thin, mum couldn't find it in her heart to play puritan.

So, Betty sat in the corner pub with her men, waiting for the siren to sound. When enough time had passed for Mrs Driver to get in, we'd hear Betty's quick, light steps and the heavier tread of men's boots – sometimes Polish, sometimes Czech, mainly plain British – as she scuttled upstairs to a world full of beds and free of judgement.

The egalitarianism of area bombing was revealed to us the morning after raids. Mum, grim-faced and apprehensive, went to the warden's hut to see the two sheets of paper that each attack placed on the coarse-nails-and-creosote wood. One was a list of the dead from the night before and this was checked first – please God, no friends or relations. Next to it was a map marked with crosses where the bombs had hit and this was scrutinised to see which parts of town had copped it.

I could see lines of craters, running straight from a bomb-aimer's view but slicing through the rigid social barriers of my young life. A single plane's bellyful could make a dot-to-dot starting in the big houses by the park, then cutting through the crescents and avenues in the better parts of town, across the roads and streets where normal people lived and on into the rougher neighbourhoods where I wasn't allowed to play.

I looked in amazement at those places that had been as distant to me as the hot and dusty lands in the two-thirds-pink atlas at school. Places rare and commonplace, familiar and forbidden, suddenly tied together by the flight of a falling bomb.

A Little Piece of Home

Joe stepped off the train and held the package close to his side. Clutching it tightly he looked up and tried to make out his surroundings through the thick acidy smoke that was billowing out from the steam train. A guard jostled him along saying "Come on Lad move away from the train now," so he moved further along the platform to avoid the crowds that were shoving and pushing, trying to get to their destination.

He was a small boy for his age, seven years old last October, he had never been on a train before, no need in London, you just walked, or if it was a special treat his Mum took him on the bus. Sharp pangs in his chest brought back the memory of yesterday when he was contently playing with his friend Billy down the street, looking for shrapnel amongst the rubble down old Victoria Street. It all seemed so long ago now.

Joe moved towards some trunks that had been stacked in a corner and sat down on the cold hard ground, hidden from any inquisitive eyes. Pulling open the package he had been tightly holding, a scorched, worse-for-wear ear popped out. Continuing to rip the package open, he held up a tatty old yellow teddy bear. One eye was missing and it had more scorch marks over its body, it gave off an unpleasant smoky stench but to Joe it was a link to his past, his home, his friends and most of all, his Mum.

She had found him with Billy and said he had to come home, that there was something she needed to talk to him about. He saw that she had been crying. Once they were back home, she sat him at the kitchen table with a small glass of milk. Gulping it down, it was then that he saw the little brown suitcase standing all alone in the hallway. It had a beige coloured label attached. His Mum saw his eyes go from the suitcase to her, questioning. She crouched down beside him and took his arms, he wasn't sure if this was for his benefit or hers.

'Joe,' she said swallowing hard. 'You're going to have to be really brave for me, you see, you're going to go and stay with a friend in the countryside'

'But we don't know anybody in the countryside Mum,' Joe tried to interrupt.

'Now Joe, don't be difficult, it's someone I know but you don't and because of all these bombings, well it's just not safe here.'

Joe looked confused, 'If it's not safe aren't you coming too then?'

His Mum stood up and turned towards the window.

'I can't Joe I have to be here for when your Father comes home, but we can write to each other and...' she then gave a small sob.

'Go and wash up now, I've laid out your clothes, we have to go soon and put you on a train, now won't that be an adventure.'

A sharp piercing whistle brought him back to the present and he buried his face into the bear's smoky, worn out fur, trying to stem the flow of tears that were falling.

Put Kettle On

Joe stepped off the train and held the package close to his side: letters and cards from Clara and his mother that he had been reading for the umpteenth time on the journey from Amiens, the poems and sketches from quiet moments by candlelight in the dugout, and some pictures of Egypt given him by Stan. His war was over: shrapnel from a shell as they moved into Bapaume had seen to that. God willing it was now nearly over for everyone. A few hours and he would be back in Blighty, then up to London: he might even make it back home for tea-time tomorrow.

At Dover he went to the Post Office to send a telegraphic message to expect him. The annoying sore throat he had developed in France had worsened and he was covered in sweat but shivering with cold.

Crossing London he collapsed and someone ran for an ambulance

Ivy was sat with Violet in the washroom at the back of Pitsmoor Post Office when Mrs Armitage, the post mistress blew her whistle. There were two jobs and Ivy had grabbed one before Violet could react.

'My turn to go to Fir Vale,' she said and thrust the envelope in the leather pouch on her belt, grinning over her shoulder at Violet's cross expression. 'Tha can go to Burngreave.'

Violet pursued her. 'I'll get thi, Ivy Wilson!'

'Have to catch us first!'

It was a lovely day outside; the early autumn sunshine meant she could still wear her straw hat: the oilskin sou'westers they wore in the rain were not exactly glamorous. But the straw hat, especially with the brim turned up – how old Armitage hated that – was quite fetching with her blonde hair tied up behind.

With any luck Ralph and his friends would be out in the park, so if she was quick – and she could rely on her long legs – she could nip to the park and be back well before Armitage's clock ran out. She knew she turned young men's heads – even navy blue serge couldn't hide her new-found curves – how they loved a uniform. It was thanks to this uniform she'd got to see the King and Queen. When the policeman held people back she had said "telegram" and they'd let her through, just in time to see the carriage go past down the Moor. The red piping and brass buttons were quite nice though. She stopped to check the buttons and gave them a quick rub with her button stick – they soon tarnished in this air.

She reached the lodge and showed the telegram to the old lodge keeper, who waved her through with a daft smile. She went up through the old workhouse to the new block housing the wounded soldiers. She handed the telegram to the ward sister, waited to see if there was a reply, then turned on her heels. She didn't have time to chat up the soldiers today; it was better in the park: even if Ralph wasn't there there'd as likely be other colonials watching the old men play bowls – feeling lost and lonely, far from home. Handsome lads who would appreciate her company, if only for the few minutes she had.

'G'day gorgeous! I was hoping my favourite girl would drop by today.' Ralph was sat on a bench with some other Australians, his trouser leg folded up where his foot once was.

'I can't stop long or I'll gerra a dobbie.'

60

'You'll what?'

'*Get – a – dobbie*: y'know – a report off t' gaffer.'

'The what? And you Poms say we don't speak English proper! Listen, when this war's over, I'll take you home with me and teach you to speak like an Aussie. What d'y say?'

Ivy knew she was blushing, knew it made her look even cuter. 'You're a right one you are! And anyhow, I'm too young to marry.' She blew them a kiss and ran off leaving the soldiers laughing behind her. She was pleased to cheer them up, poor things. All these handsome men, with scars and bits missing. She hoped there would still be whole ones left.

What a terrible thing war was! Though she had had such an adventure herself, one that wouldn't have happened without the war. She was ashamed to say she had thoroughly enjoyed it and it had not affected her like it had some: her father was irreplaceable at Vickers, designing guns or something, and, joy of joys, her big brother Joe was safe and on his way back. Only yesterday a telegram had arrived; she had taken it herself – her mother had said "if ever one arrives for me, will you bring it, our Ivy; I'd rather you bring it than a stranger." It was with some trepidation that she'd carried it home. Should she open it? It was strictly against the rules – it meant an instant sacking – and perhaps it would bring bad luck. She'd played it cool with her mother, and tried not to let her see her trembling fingers when she'd asked her to open it. "It's all right mother, it says – "Reached Dover. Put kettle on for tea tomorrow. Buy pikelets. Joe – " She was on eight while four today, so would be back to welcome him home.

Half of the time those telegrams were not such good

news. Distress telegrams they called them. Often you'd find the women grouped in the yard, like they knew that news was on its way. Her arrival brought a hush until they heard who it was for. A lot of them wanted her to open it for them and to read it – either they were too scared or couldn't read. She hated reading them out. Like being in school. And how *was* she supposed to read out the "serving King and country" ones? They were not allowed to stay and offer comfort, which was a relief, that was what neighbours were for.

Yes, that was the only bad bit about the job. She would be sad in a way when it was over – when the boys came back and wanted their jobs back. When she'd started there were still some boys doing the job, but they soon all went away. Even when the Zeppelins were coming over they had still gone out and done their job: she hadn't been afraid. Although there was that time she'd taken the short cut across the fields to Southey in the dark. Her lantern only cast enough light to read an address on a telegram or a door number – being designed for the blackout. Then she'd come to a guard next to the searchlight and big gun. "Halt! Who goes there!" he'd said. "Me," she'd squeaked as he was threatening to shoot her. "Telegram," she'd spluttered.

What would she do after the war to earn twenty shillings? What if Ralph was serious in his offer – what would Australia be like? A fresh start. And it was, after all, only his foot missing – so far as she knew. Who knows what the future brings?

She arrived back at the washroom and Violet had the kettle over the fire.

'Tha's an angel Vi,' she said.

'Unlike thi,' Violet jabbed back, grinning. 'Were they

there?'

'Maybe. Two sugars please.'

'Sugar! If only! Anyhow don't change the subject. My turn next.'

'Of course Violet. Of course.' She blew steam from the cup. 'What's tha reckon to Ralph, the blonde one?'

The whistle blew outside. Violet jumped up. She returned looking drained, holding an envelope. 'Ivy, it's for thi mother...'

No Home in This World

Joe stepped off the plane and held the package close to his chest. After almost two years in a cold, wet foreign climate, the tropical heat almost took his breath away. Minutes after disembarking, sweat was running into his eyes making them sting, his body was sticky and his hands clammy. When he first arrived in Scotland, claiming asylum, he thought he'd never get used to weather; now he longed for the bracing horizontal rain.

They were waiting for him. They took his bag, and put handcuffs on him.

'Please,' he said, 'my pills are in the bag. Without them, I…'

The slap across his cheek silenced him. He knew what these men were capable of: he'd seen them in action. Police whose idea of law and order was to treat everyone as guilty: beat them, torture them, if necessary shoot them. Joe knew they thought his sort were less than human, and he'd seen how they treated animals.

He was bundled into the back of a van, chained to a rail and locked in. There was no window. The van drove away, rattling over the potholes, its horn sometimes blasting at what he assumed were other road users, the van occasionally breaking suddenly. Over the noise of the ageing van he could hear the radio broadcasting Afrobeat, Reggae and Hip Hop at full volume. He felt the beginning of a headache, and he was in danger of being sick. The music made way for the news headlines. Apparently, government soldiers were attempting to stop Muslims travelling to Christian areas, and Christians from entering Muslim areas in an attempt to control the escalating sectarian violence. Both a mosque and a church had been bombed, with much loss of life.

Before being deported from Scotland he had gone online and, as he suspected, little had changed. Despite a new leader, the government remained in chaos and the secular courts were in disarray, the vacuum being filled by preachers and imams. He shook his head. The conflict between the fundamentalists on both sides didn't make any sense to him, particularly as they both agreed on so much – including their disgust and horror at people like him.

He must have dozed off: he was wakened by a kick in his shins. He was unchained from the rail, had the handcuffs reattached and was dragged off the burning hot van into the hot and humid street, from where he was taken into an official-looking building. He recognised it. He had been interrogated here years ago. It hadn't changed much: the walls were still a dirty grey, the tables and chairs screwed to the floor. It still smelled of the cheap disinfectant that failed to hide the stink of piss, shit and vomit.

He was taken to an airless, windowless room, containing a table and two chairs. He was chained to one of the chairs. Then he was left.

His mind went back to his failed attempt at getting asylum. When he arrived in Scotland – hidden in the back of a truck – he found himself bewildered by Glasgow. And he could hardly understand a word that was said to him: it seemed to him the Scots spoke a peculiar sort of English. Still, they were friendly. He was shown the way to an advice centre where the staff arranged everything, including temporary accommodation in a high rise flat. They provided him with a lawyer who helped him with the asylum application.

His reverie was interrupted when a familiar figure entered the room. So the lieutenant was still here, despite the change of government and general instability. Tall, well built with piercing eyes and a lack of any hair on his face and head, he towered over Joe.

He grinned. 'Well, Joe, we meet again?' He pointed to the spare chair, asking: 'May I?'

Joe shrugged. 'I'm not in a position to stop you.'

The lieutenant sat down. 'Now, Joe, don't be like that. As you've returned to us, perhaps we can be friends.'

'I'm not here voluntarily.'

The lieutenant scratched his bald pate. 'Yes, I heard you were chucked out of England.'

'It wasn't England, it was Scotland.'

'Whatever. It does seem wherever you go, you fall out with people. Doesn't that tell you something?'

Joe tried to keep his expression blank. But inside he was in turmoil. He was angry at the treatment he had received. He was scared of what would happen now. He was hungry and thirsty. And the pain in his body told him he should have taken his pills sometime ago. Eventually, he spoke.

'Can I have my medication back please? I can't function without it.'

The lieutenant shook his head. 'What are we going to do with you? Free you and let you continue with your behaviour? Put you in prison with others of your kind? Send you to a mental hospital?'

'It's not my mind that's ill, it's my body. That's why I need my pills.'

'Oh, but it is your mind as well. Look, I'll get you your pills, just as soon as I see some sign of you co-operating.'

'I don't know what you want. I don't know what I can tell you. All I want to do is live my life, be what I am.'

'Joe, Joe, but don't you see that is the problem. Surely you know we can't let you live your life as you are. Let's face it, you're a criminal. We wouldn't let murderers and rapists and thieves go free and be themselves, now would we? Surely you must realise that.'

'I'm not a murderer. I don't do any harm to anyone, do I?'

'But Joe, you do harm others. You corrupt others. And you spread disease. And dissent. And your sort incite violence.' He raised his hand. 'Now don't interrupt Joe. I know your sort claim you don't mean to incite violence and I know you claim to be the victims, but that is just semantics. Just semantics. Because you do incite violence.'

Joe remained silent.

After several minutes, the lieutenant stood up. 'Have it your own way, Joe. I'll leave you to think about it. I'll come back in a couple of hours. Perhaps then you'll co-operate. And then you can have your medication back. Joe, think about it.' He left, locking the door after him.

It could all have been so different, he thought, if only the authorities had believed he was an asylum seeker. They treated him as an economic migrant. He wasn't allowed to work, even though there was a shortage of teachers. Instead, he helped other migrants to understand English, taught them the rudiments of the language so they would know what was being said to them, so they could understand questions on forms.

His lawyer tried everything. But the authorities just wouldn't believe him. They had even found some Glasgow prostitute who told them he had had sex with her. He shook his head. He'd never met her, didn't know who she was. Perhaps she'd been bribed, he wasn't sure if bribery occurred in Scotland. It certainly did back home.

The pain in his body was excruciating, was getting worse. He clenched his teeth so he wouldn't cry out: he wouldn't give them the satisfaction.

The thugs in power here certainly believed him. That was why they had thrown him in prison, that was why he escaped to another country. But the authorities over there hadn't believed him, or claimed not to. Perhaps they were just looking for an excuse to deport him.

One day, early in the morning, the police came round and took him to Dungavel where he was kept until he was put on a plane back to the homeland that had mistreated him all his adult life.

He realised he had no choice. He had dozed off, but was woken by the pain, which was now almost unbearable. The lack of food and water was weakening his body's ability to fight the pain. He screamed.

The lieutenant returned. 'Are you prepared to co-operate now?'

Joe nodded. He knew from his past experiences the sequence of events. He would give the lieutenant a blow job. He would then get his medication back, as well as food and drink. Afterwards? He didn't know. Perhaps he'd be kept in prison where he'd probably be raped over and over. Or they might release him and follow him, hoping he'd lead them to others. Or conscript him, sending him to the front to help keep the warring fundamentalists apart. Perhaps some queer bashers would kill him.

Sacrifice

Jo stepped off the train, holding the package close to her chest. She was surprised that it hadn't melted into her skin the way she'd been holding it so tightly for the whole journey. The three people seated across from her in the six-seater compartment of the old steam train, had sent occasional quizzical looks in her direction but this might also have been because of her clothes or because of her striking white blonde hair and cornflower blue eyes. She had tried so hard to find suitable clothes for this trip to London but could see as soon as she stepped into the carriage that she had failed. There had been much chat about the war and the fact that Hitler's armies were getting too close for comfort. There had been such hope the previous June. So much for "Careless Talk" and all that. Despair was taking over. She shuddered. She knew this all too well. For the last part of the journey she hadn't been feeling too good as it was, her head ached and she felt feverish. It wasn't a good sign, but perhaps it was just a coincidence and she had caught flu.

Now, in Euston Station, The Royal Scot hissing like some mediaeval dragon, she hailed a taxi and asked to be taken to the address she'd managed to find in the archives at Mitchell Library in Glasgow. She'd spent every day there for a week since she'd received her great uncle's papers the week before. Her great-grandfather's brother, "Uncle Jack," a relation she had never known she had, had died in February 1945. What he had written had shocked her to the core and she had known that she had to do something immediately.

The taxi driver deposited her in a Regency square with railings closing off a private park. It was so tranquil that it was hard to imagine the hell that she knew was breaking loose across Europe. As with the train fare, she was amazed at how little it cost. She gave him a tip, probably too large by the look of delight on his face. She had been lucky that her grandfather had collected old coins! He tipped his old, worn cap at her and told her to be careful, to go to the nearest air raid shelter if she heard the sirens.

A light snow was falling, floating softly down on her face as she looked for the number of the house.

She went slowly up the steps, wondering for the thousandth time how she was going to explain her mission and her package. She sensed she didn't have long – she felt an acute pain in her abdomen. It was not like any illness she had had before. She pulled on the bell pull and heard a ringing some way off. She hoped to God that he would be in, she didn't have time to be trailing round London. Had her research paid off? Had she found the right man?

'I've come to see the Air Vice-Marshall,' she said when a tall thin man, evidently a butler, opened the door.

'I'm sorry, Miss, but there is no such person...'

She knew his type, men like him hadn't changed.

'I've no time for this, the outcome of this war depends on you letting me past. Do you want to be personally responsible for the deaths of millions of people, and the destruction of this city?'

He was clearly taken back by such a forthright approach from a woman. As he stuttered, she took advantage and pushed past him.

Inside was an oak panelled entrance hall where a distinguished-looking man with a fine moustache was buttoning his overcoat. She recognised him from the old photo in the archives. Air Vice-Marshall Thripps.

'What the blazes! Who are you? How dare you come

71

barging in here!'

'Sir, I don't have long. I have information for you from Special Ops Sigma.'

'How do you know… W-what?'

'It's vital, sir, it's about the A-bomb.'

He looked stunned. 'You'd better come through.'

He removed his coat and led her through into a library where he sat down behind a leather topped desk. He indicated a chair opposite. She thrust her package at him, saying, breathlessly: 'I can't make you take this seriously but please, please do. The future of Britain depends on what you do now.'

Bemused, the man sat down and picked up the small package, almost gingerly as if he expected it to be booby-trapped. He extricated a diary and a notebook.

He sat in silence reading for some time as she gazed out at the plane trees in the square swaying as the wind swirled flurries of snowflakes. He looked up at her.

'Where on earth did you get this?'

Jo coughed. She held her chest where she felt the pain that had been there for some hours now.

'My great uncle left it to me, in his will,' she said.

'But it's dated February 1945. Next month,' he said. 'Why did he put a future date on it?'

This was the hard part.

'He wrote it next month, in February. As you no doubt know, Special Operations Sigma are under deep cover in Germany.'

'But no one knows that.'

She continued. 'Please, just listen. My relative got in on the German Atom bomb project facility, the *Uranprojekt* – the details are there. They are now just weeks away from having the capability and will launch more deadly V2s than you can ever imagine – unless you act swiftly to destroy them.'

'But, what do you mean, he wrote it *next* month? Do you mean he predated it? Why?'

'I'll try to explain that later. You'll see that the postscript in the notebook mentions a prisoner of war camp. My relative was apparently captured not long after he wrote this. He doesn't say how he managed to hide or keep the information stored in those two…'

She pointed at the diary and notebook but remained silent as once again her body was wracked by coughing, and another sharp pain in her belly made her gasp.'

'Are you all right, Miss? Can I get you a glass of water?'

'He must have passed the information to someone knowing he was to be caught. Perhaps in the hope they could get the information back in time.'

'But how could he be captured after today's date?'

Jo looked at him, desperate tears welling up in her blue eyes. She pushed her white blonde hair out of her eyes.

'I don't know how to make you understand this, Sir but…"

She took a deep breath.

'I come from Britain in the year 2045. I live in Schottland, that's what we have to call it now, in Glasgow, the German capital of Britain. London was obliterated. That was only the start of it. Germany won the war you call the Second World War. We had no choice but to surrender after the bombs. Once London and Churchill were vapourised the nation lost heart. Much of Britain has never been rebuilt after the terrible bombings. Near where I live, in Glasgow, Clydebank was badly hit in the second Blitz. The ruined buildings and bomb craters are still there, left as a warning, I believe, to us, to never dare to wage war against the master race again. The German mark is our currency. Queen Elizabeth died in prison forty years ago. The Cold War between the Germanic States and America has exacerbated the terrible persecutions. In my parents' time, it was the rounding up and imprisonment and murder of Jews and anyone deemed to have a skin that was too dark. In my time, this has escalated to include people with dark hair or brown eyes. My neighbour was removed in the night last year and never seen again.'

'London destroyed? Surrendered?' asked the confused man in front of her.

'I'm sorry, Sir. I know it's a lot to take in, but I am serious.' Tears now ran down her cheeks. The pain was intensifying.

She took a deep breath and continued.

'Only those thought to be part of The Fuhrer's perfect Aryan race were allowed to have further education after the age of twelve.'

The man behind the desk was looking seriously alarmed. She was still not sure he was convinced, she feared he would call for help to have her arrested.

'Uncle Jack said in his letter that his findings and those of his team would enable Britain and her allies to win the war. He must have lost his mind or his memory after this and the notebook and diary didn't get posted. I don't know where they went after his death. All I know is that it came to me from a very elderly woman who found it in her father's possessions which didn't reach her for years after he had died.

'I can't explain the course of events which led to the non- discovery of this package till it reached me. The woman's daughter had looked up his family tree on the internet... I'm sorry... you will have no idea what I am talking about, Sir. In our 21st century world we have machines called computers which give us information, a bit like the wireless and the British Library combined. I belong to a special research institute that works to the direction of the current Führer. We are experimenting with the ability to travel backwards in time. It has worked partially with rats, but never tried on humans before, not even on untermensch – until I broke through the security systems to try it on myself. Being blonde and blue-eyed, I was given further education and I work in the Führer's time lab. This coincidence made me believe that all this had happened for a purpose. Anyway you don't need to know all this.

'I've taken the risk of travelling back to give you this package in the hope that you will use the information it contains to beat Hitler and take the future of Britain into your own hands. I know I can't travel forward to my own time again but I have no close family as my parents died in a car crash last year and I have no brothers or sisters. I felt it right to take the risk for the freedom and happiness of so many yet to be born.'

The pain was all through her body. Excruciating. She felt she was going to be sick. She stood up, unsteadily and made for the door.

The Air Vice-Marshall let her go. If she was correct in what she had said, there was no conceivable way he could help her. He started to read through the notebook and diary pages once again.

There was a screech of brakes outside and a loud banging noise. He jumped to his feet and ran to the window. A red London bus had stopped suddenly but not in time to avoid the female figure in bizarre clothes. He flung up the window, letting in a flurry of snowflakes.

'Good God man, what happened?' he shouted to the driver who had got out of his bus and was standing looking helplessly down.

'Guv, she just staggered out onto the road. I couldn't help but hit her.'

The autopsy on the young woman showed that inside she had been almost disintegrating. The vital organs had – "withered" – that was the description given by the pathologist. The bus driver was absolved of all blame. Whether or not Jo had deliberately gone in front of the bus would never be known.

The Germans were pushed back and surrendered, and peace came to Britain and Europe in May 1945.

*

Peter and Mary McDonald who lived in Glasgow were delighted when the war ended and Peter came home unscathed from the battlefields. Their joy was complete when nine months later, their daughter, Susan, was born. She in turn, living in a world of peace and prosperity, married her Jewish boyfriend in 1971. There third child was a daughter, Jane who grew up to have a successful career in medical research. In 2015 she became pregnant with twins following IVF. In a Glasgow maternity home, Jane gave birth to identical twin girls. Joy turned to sadness on being told that one little girl had been stillborn. They named her Joanne and her twin sister, Josephine. Josephine, taking after her mother, grew up with white blonde hair and cornflower blue eyes.

Charity Shop Shoes

Abdul stretched, letting out a relieved groan. His Kalashnikov hung from his back. He wore Pashtun dress and old worn out shoes. A ragged turban, that hung loose, covered his head.

The powerful, rugged, white-tipped mountains surrounded him. Many light coloured scars cut through the dark, earthly rock like roots. An eagle nonchalantly floated in the clear blue sky, its wings outstretched looking for prey.

This had been the home of his people for thousands of years. He had never known peace, nor had his father or his father's father. His eyes fixed on a spot in the far-off mountains, like dark pebbles, his eye lashes occasionally blinking, his lips shut tight.

He re-entered his home. Asifa, his wife, was preparing the food and his son Ramjad and young daughter Matilda were amusing themselves on the floor. Their home was typical of all the village's habitats, it was made from stone with wooden roofs and doors. It was basic inside with hammocks for the children and a large base that was made from wood and scrap metal that acted as the adult's bed. They had a covering made from sheep and camel wool which kept them warm during the long winters. There was an open fire which served a dual purpose of preparing food and keeping them warm. The family ate their food on the floor, sat on beautifully woven mats, which was the tradition.

Asifa was dressed in a long, loose-fitting, brightly-coloured dress with a tight fitting head scarf. Her complexion was fresh and free of any worry lines, which gave the impression that she was much younger than her husband.

Abdul's thoughts returned to the moment. He breathed in the smell of fresh bread.

'Asifa you make the best bread in the whole village.'

She turned and looked at her husband.

'My father used to say the same thing to my mother, we Hassen's are renowned for our bread.'

'That's why I married you.'

'You married me just for my bread!'

'No, your beauty and wisdom as well!'

'Ramjad help your sister prepare for food.'

Matilda was struggling to pour the water from the large jug into a small saucer to wash her hands. The little child was a miniature of her mother, wearing a brightly coloured dress but without the head scarf. She had wild, black hair and big dark eyes.

Ramjad took the jug from the little girl and poured the water for her. He then got up and went over to his father.

'Father, are you going to fight again today?' he asked.

'Yes, son.'

Ramjad stood still, his arms by his sides.

'When will the fighting end, father?'

Abdul placed his large hands on the boy's small shoulders.

'It will never end, Ramjad. My father fought the British and his father and his father's father fought the British and two hundred years later we are still fighting the British and also the Americans.'

Ramjad's face was serious in thought, his mind thirsty for information.

'The food is ready,' Asifa said.

Abdul went and took his place in the circle, Ramjad

followed, his head bowed. The two sat down. Abdul
started to eat his food. Ramjad sat still – a pensive look on
his face.

'Why don't people leave us alone Father?'

Abdul pulled at the bread and scooped up some rice.
He took his time to answer his son.

'We have natural resources, mainly oil which the
Americans and British want. They are scared the Russians
will be back again and take all the oil.'

'Ramjad eat your food, the bread will be cold,' Asifa
said.

Life was very hard. They tried to grow vegetables but
the land was too harsh and barren for growing anything.
Abdul rose from the circle. He was tall, well over six foot,
and slim. Ramjad craned his neck to look at him.

'You won't die will you, Father.'

'We all die someday, Ramjad. The most important thing
is to die a free spirit and not under the power of another
man. We are a very resilient and proud people. It has not
always been like this. We were once very wealthy and lived
good lives.'

'What do you mean father?'

'I mean we always had enough food for our stomachs.
We lived down in the towns during the British Empire and
would trade leather and many other goods with our Indian
neighbours. We lived peacefully until the British started
coming over the border and trying to control us and claim
all the natural resources for themselves. We fought back
but we were no match for them and were driven out of
our homes and forced to flee to the mountains where we
have lived ever since.'

Asifa did her work, accentuating the noise to show her
annoyance at the conversation which she had heard many

times.

'I want to fight when I get older!' Ramjad's face lit up as though a great idea had just come into his head.

Abdul looked at his son as though he was about to admonish him.

'You concentrate on those books I brought back for you, and hopefully one day you'll become a doctor and you will leave this village for a better place,' he looked at Asifa, as though he was seeking her approval.

He opened the door and walked outside; Asifa quickly followed.

'Why do you say those things to him, you know we can't afford to send him to university.'

'We have to believe there is a better future for Ramjad, that is what spurns me on, the thought we will drive the British and Americans out of our country and we can move back into the towns, then I can get a better-paid job and be able to afford to send him to university,' he stared intensely at her.

'I have to go Asifa,' and he kissed her gently on the lips.

He joined up with a party of other local men. Their job was to control their designated area looking out for enemy patrols or trucks ferrying troops or supplies between bases.

The crazy thing about this current war that made him despair, was that they had once been friends with the British in their fight against the Russians and he often thought about the time he invited a British soldier back to his home and the soldier offering him the same hospitality.

They trudged through the jagged and loose rocks to their look-out post. They all wore the Pashtun dress and headgear and old shoes that looked like they had been purchased from some back street charity shop in England.

Without their obligatory Kalashnikovs and rocket launchers, they would look just like goat herders.

'Yousef, you remember the time we all invited British soldiers back to our village, we had a whole platoon of them. I remember his face now, he had the hair that had seen too much sun and eyes like our sky on a perfect sunny day. His name was Davis and he said to me when we defeated the Russians, my family and I would have to visit him in England, he said *Stock in the Trent*, it was a funny name.'

Yousef did not answer, nor did the other men, their heads down and lost in thought. They finally reached their destination and perched themselves on a large piece of jutting rock. The position gave them a perfect view of the main road from Kabul to Kandahar and they could launch their rockets at any British or American convoys, and at the same time be out of reach of returning fire. The only thing they feared were the American jets that would indiscriminately bomb anything that moved or any buildings standing after such attacks. He was always fearful for his family and had discovered a cave nearby to where they lived and had instructed Asifa to take the children into the cave should she hear planes overhead. He had seen whole villages wiped out by these flying Dragons, they would call them. Men, women, children and babies, their bodies resembling burnt wood, their arms stiff and raised in front of them as though they would protect them. The black skeleton faces always looked the same – mouths wide open with large white teeth and starey eyes as though they had just seen the devil.

The men took out their small metal containers that had rice and chickpeas, and maybe some bread if they were lucky. They ate their food with their fingers, not taking their eyes off the road. Silence engulfed them, they never spoke while they were on look-out – an echoing voice could be heard five miles away, even a whisper.

He contemplated what Asifa had said to him. He desperately wanted a better life for his children – to see his family in a better and safer place where his children could flourish was all he wished for. A vision had come to him in his sleep that he would die a martyr like many brothers before him, so he was determined somehow to get his family out of Afghanistan before he died.

The beauty of the land that surrounded him was always inspiring. The landscape had not changed in thousands of years. A large expanse of rock of different shades and shapes. If you stared long enough at the rock, you could make out faces, maybe dead warriors from the past that had been swallowed up by this enigmatic mass. The mountains would give him strength. He wished his family could just turn into rock people and go and blend in with the rest of the rock and be left alone to lead their lives how they see fit.

He was lost in this reverie when all of a sudden he heard a truck approaching. One of the men with a rocket launcher, took aim. Within seconds the truck was blown apart and bodies lay strewn on the road side. They steadily clambered down the rocks, their guns aimed at the carnage.

Towards the back of the burnt out shell of the truck, a groan could be heard; Abdul went to investigate – there was a British soldier sprawled out. He raised his gun in preparation for finishing off the enemy.

'Help me!' the soldier muttered.

He looked at the soldier, his finger was tense on the trigger. He was a split second away from pulling the trigger, when all he could see was Davis, his friend of so many years ago looking at him. It was as though he had come back.

'Name!' he demanded.

'Davis, Private Davis, please don't kill me I have three young children!'

He lowered his gun, his heart felt like it would jump out of his chest, and quickly fumbled around in his waistcoat pocket and took out a photo he had of Davis with his wife and two very young boys. It had his address on the back and he had kept it, hoping if his prayers were answered he may visit him one day in England. No one, not even Asifa, knew of this photo. He showed it to the British soldier and pointed at Davis.

'It's my Dad!' the soldier said.

He knew a smattering of English words that Davis had taught him. He wracked his brain, his face contorted in concentration trying to think of the word.

'Father!' he frantically nodded his head pointing at the man in the photo.

'Yes!' the soldier also nodded his head.

He could hear the footsteps of his comrades approaching, his chest felt like it was encapsulated in a tight metal cover; his head felt like it would explode.

'Abdul, why you not shoot the British soldier?' Yousef said

'I can't.'

'Stand clear, then I will.'

'No!' and he barred his way.

Yousef and the rest of Abdul's comrades stared at him as though the prophet Mohammed was sitting on his shoulders.

'Abdul, we need to kill the enemy, what is wrong!'

'He is the son of Davis, I had a connection with that man that I have never felt outside our village. He was a good man, he did not want war either, like us. I am going to take him back to their camp.'

He had already made up his mind and picked up the soldier and threw the man's arm over his shoulder. Groans could be heard from the semi-conscious man.

'Abdul, you know the Chieftains will have you killed when you get back.'

Yousef's voice was lost to him, he was focussed only on helping the soldier; his face grimaced with the strain of holding up the weight of man, as he headed off along the tarmac road.

He walked for fifteen miles with the injured soldier, shouting constantly at him in the limited English he knew to keep him awake, before he was finally spotted by another British patrol and taken back to their camp.

The soldier was badly injured but he survived. Abdul was kept in the British compound for a few weeks where he was treated well, given good food and taught some more English. He visited the soldier many times in the field hospital and the two developed a good friendship sharing their stories about Davis.

One day, in the hospital, he was told that there was a surprise for him, and in walked Davis who he hadn't seen for over thirty years. He still looked the same with the sun drenched hair and sky blue eyes but there were some grey tinges in his hair now.

The two men renewed their friendship, and Davis explained that he had saved his son's life and he wanted to help him in some way.

'My family, please take my family back to England and make sure they have a good education,' Abdul said.

It would be a very hard task to pull off but they had to try. They agreed that he would have to secretly go back to the village where he would collect his family. A truck would be waiting on the main road where they would be picked up.

So he disguised himself as an old man and made his way back to his village.

He finally arrived back at his house after five hours of walking. He was nervous and slowly opened the door and peered inside. Asifa and the children were just finishing their food and did not notice him.

'Quickly Asifa, it is me, we have to go!'

'What have you done Abdul, you know they will kill you!'

'There's no time, we must go!'

The family quickly gathered a few personal possessions then left for the road.

When they eventually reached the pick-up point, it was in the middle of the night, the truck was already waiting with all its lights turned off. Abdul lifted his family on to the truck.

'Abdul come on, what are you waiting for!' Asifa said.

'I am not going, this is my home. I have seen my dream come alive of seeing my family have a better life.'

'Abdul, get on the truck, they will kill you!' Davis said.

He ignored the words, and went closer to Ramjad and Matilda.

'Ramjad you be good, and look after your mother, study hard and be a good man.'

Ramjad had tears in his eyes.

'Father, why don't you come with us?'

'I would be leaving my Father, and my Father's father. Their spirits are still here and so must I be.'

He scanned the large black shapes of the mountains. The sky was a charcoal black, the myriad stars flickered.

'I will stay also,' Asifa said, as she climbed down from the truck.

Matilda held out her arms for her mother and started to cry.

Davis comforted the two children who were now both crying and pleading for their parents.

'The children need their parents,' Davis said.

'The children have not known war for long, they are still young and will be able to adapt to the Western world. I have seen and heard too much, I am like the rain god who is suddenly told to cast sun from his hands,' Asifa said.

'She is right Davis, we belong here, this is our home, please look after my children and maybe one day we'll all meet again,' he said.

'Don't worry about your children Abdul, I will care for them like they are my own.'

Abdul and Asifa embraced the two children and kissed them one last time before the truck left quickly, the muffled crying could be heard from the two children in the distance.

The couple held hands.

Abdul had seen his dream come true, a better life for his children, he looked towards the sky and then at Asifa.

'You are stubborn Asifa, always have been, you should have gone with them.'

'Who would have cooked your bread, Abdul Jamal!'

The next day Abdul's and Asifa's bodies were found on the side of the mountain with a single bullet hole in each of their heads. They had both now become one of the lost warriors that had been swallowed up by the rock.

When Nigeria won independence it had a federal constitution comprising three regions defined by the principal ethnic groups in the country - the Hausa and Fulani in the north, Yoruba in the south-west, and Igbo in the south-east. As the military took over in the mid-1960s, and the economic situation worsened, ethnic tensions broke out. Tens of thousands of Igbos were killed in what has been described as genocide and up to a million fled to the Eastern Region. In May, 1967, the head of the Eastern Region, Colonel Emeka Ojukwu, unilaterally declared the independent Republic of Biafra. The ensuing civil war saw a million civilians die in fighting and from famine caused by a blockade.

The War Continues

A green military truck, in camouflage, and full of soldiers, runs amok in the streets of Lagos. The truck violates all traffic laws, and runs red lights. Two soldiers sit at the tail end of the truck, with long whips, which they use in clearing the road, by whipping people and cars out of their way as they speed on recklessly. Cars swerve, and people fall into gutters when they try to avoid the soldiers' whips.

The soldiers make rapid incursions into different nightclubs in Lagos, searching for something or someone. On their third stop, they all jump out of the truck – five of them – and rush into the club, still whipping people as they crash in. They search the club feverishly, and then come to an abrupt stop. They have found their victim: a young Igbo girl – a singer in the club.

But someone spots them and has gone to warn the singer about their presence. There is a momentary stand-off as they look at her and she looks back across the crowded dance floor. They argue among themselves about what to do, whether to just seize her and run? Her band have seen them too. They continue to play, and she continues to sing, but they are all alert to the danger and watch for the soldiers to make their move. Sensing trouble, the nightclubbers start to quietly but quickly leave the premises.

The singer seizes her opportunity in the confusion to slip away through the back door, and they lose sight of her. She could be anywhere in the maze into which she has melted away. They scratch their heads and leave.

The following day, Ijeoma enters the office of the Army Chief of Staff, and surrenders herself. The Chief already knows that she is around and is waiting for her. As soon as she enters the Chief storms out at her, pushing under her nose a letter she wrote which the authorities intercepted. The dangerous sentence in the letter reads, "Brother, I have already told you that I can only help you by remaining here," and this is something for her to explain. However, they don't let her explain; rather, she is rough-handled and locked up.

The next day, she is in the Chief's office again being interrogated. It happened that as they dragged her off to lock her up, she asked to be allowed to sing to entertain the Nigerian soldiers at the war front. The army doesn't trust her. They don't trust her intentions. What is she up to? What is her game?

The Chief of Staff, Major General Salami, calls for Colonel Ejor, the man in charge of the army detention unit, to discuss the fate of the singer.

Colonel Ejor tries to convince the Major General; 'Sir, as long as we have her under watch, I think we should allow her to entertain the officers. It could be a welcome distraction for the boys. She does have a wonderful voice.'

'What about that letter we intercepted?'

'We transferred her brother to an unknown location as soon as we found out that his former place of consignment had been compromised, Sir.'

'Do you not think that's why she's willing to leave Lagos? That girl could be a spy.'

'I don't think so, Sir. She's just an entertainer. We have no real case for detaining her. At least this way we can keep an eye on her.'

'Well, I leave it to you, then, to coordinate things. Be careful not to botch things again this time.'

'Sir, I can assure you, she will have no place to hide. I will keep a special eye on her.'

In the meantime, at the detention unit, word leaks out that Ijeoma, the famous singer, is being detained there. From cell to cell, the whisper is passed of her presence. Detainees seek for ways of making contact with her. Most detainees are people like her, detained for one political offence or another, or people the military want out of the way until the fever of the recent coup calms down. Ijeoma's brother was a Lieutenant General in the government that just toppled, and he – like all his colleagues – is in detention.

Ijeoma had used her singing to help a number of the members of the old regime to leave the country and head to safety. Her singing brings her in contact with people of high social standing, and she gets to know things. She also uses her art to inquire and find out about things; then her craft to divulge her findings through song to those they are meant for. So, to some extent, she could be considered a spy. But she knows they have nothing on her.

Ijeoma always has a lookout when she performs, especially when she sings her "telling" songs. As soon as these lookouts sight someone that looks like, or is suspected to be, a law enforcement person, whether in uniform or not, they signal Ijeoma, and the words of her song shift from "telling" to singing non-compromising words.

During a break at the detention unit, one detainee seeks out Ijeoma and both of them have a happy reunion. Benson is also a singer like Ijeoma. He had disappeared from circulation for months and no one knew what had happened to him. Quickly, he tells Ijeoma about his predicament. According to him, the daughter of one of the top military officers accused him of rape. He denied it, of course, but the girl is pregnant.

'Did you do it Benson?'

'I don't know, really, I don't know.' He scratches his head in desperation. 'I told the father that I will marry the daughter. But I didn't rape her.'

Ijeoma smiles. 'So, he keeps you here until he decides whether to let you marry his daughter?'

Benson doesn't reply. He is pensive, though, rather than worried. 'What about you? What are they holding you for?'

'They think I'm a spy,' she says.

'A spy? Phaw! As if they will tell one if they see a spy.'

Some warders are eavesdropping on her conversation. She doesn't know whether they are doing it for curiosity as her fans, or to spy on her. She smiles and a wicked gleam brightens her eyes. 'So...' she says, 'I want them to send me to the front... I want to perform for the soldiers.' She knows the power of her singing. She has used it before, and feels confident to use it again.

While they talk, a Black Maria pulls up nearby. Prisoners peep through the small barred windows of the truck.

'Biafran Soldiers!' Benson says with a hiss.

'Not likely.' Ijeoma frowns at Benson. 'Why would you think that? Which side are you on?'

'Sorry, Ije. That's the way they transport them.'

Benson is Yoruba, and the issue of Biafra is a no go area for Ijeoma. Benson should never have joked about it; that is, if he *was* joking. Henceforth, Ijeoma stays away from Benson.

Back at the Chief of Staff's office, the Colonel tries once more to convince the Chief to allow Ijeoma to perform for the soldiers. But the Chief continues to hammer on about the letter Ijeoma wrote. He believes Ijeoma is a risk that they'd better keep in check.

The Chief of Staff does his weekly inspection at the Bonny camp. His are always surprise visits to the boys to see exactly how things work at the camp when senior officers are not around. He hears one of Ijeoma's songs on the radio, blasting over the loudspeaker at the officer's mess. He walks in and sees his officers listening with rapt attention to the song – some dancing to it. He sees the effect of Ijeoma's song on his boys, and even his normally down-turned mouth rises a little at the corner. There and then he decides to allow Ijeoma to perform for them. He believes that a live performance will do the boys good.

And so, Ijeoma performs for the Nigerian soldiers. The soldiers warm to her. She has seen them in battle, and they have seen her in performance. In short, each to their job. They fight, she performs, and the camaraderie amongst them is such that one cannot understand why there is a war, nor what they are fighting for, or why brothers should pitch against one another. She sees how, during a lull in the periods of fighting, soldiers from the different camps exchange goodies, and mix and socialize. She also sees how, at the height of war, the same soldiers change and become animals, with red-shot eyes, seeing nothing but kill, kill, kill.

Soldiers always flank her, as if to protect her, but she knows better. She knows those soldiers are under orders to watch her. They still do not trust her.

One evening, during one of the peaks in fighting, the Nigerian side is pressed hard, and forced to retreat. Confusion reigns everywhere. Again, Ijeoma seizes her opportunity to slide away – into the Biafran side – allowing herself to be captured. They take her, bind her hands and feet, and blindfold her, then take her on a long drive to their camp.

They take her to their commander. 'We caught their spy, Commander. She pretends to be a singer, but she carries messages to and fro with her songs. We know about her.'

'Then untie her and let her sing for us.' The Commander taunts her, 'I hope you can tell us all we want to know, lady.'

They untie her, and the Commander freezes. She too gapes at him in shock. Without a word, she runs and jumps on the Commander, and flings her arms around his neck. The soldiers cock their guns, but just as quickly lower them again when they see their Commander and their captive hugging and jumping up and down. This is Efuna, her brother.

'Yes, she is the singer,' her brother says and puts her down. Then he steps back and takes a good look at her.

'Boys! At ease. She is the singer who sang me and many of our people out the other side to safety. Now, Sis, you will tell me all you know, after you have rested. You are safe now.'

Against her brother's advice, she decides to entertain the head of the Biafran State. Her desire is to use her skills to make a difference in the war. After the performance, they put her in charge of a camp where children taken out of the Biafran war-zone are harboured, on the Ivory Coast. About five hundred children live in this camp. To get to Abidjan, they smuggle her out of the Biafran headquarters in Enugu early that morning on one of the relief planes. A military van picks her up at the airport and takes her through the town to the camp where the children are placed.

The camp used to be an army camp. They moved the soldiers to make way for the Biafran refugees. The camp has a huge gate with inscriptions in French. Ijeoma doesn't speak or read French, and so ignores the inscription. Hence she doesn't get the name of the camp. The camp doesn't look as if the soldiers ever lived there. It has no running water and no toilets, and for a kitchen, they have a makeshift barn, where the local women and men cook for the children. Flies swarm everywhere – big green-eyed flies buzzing about and perching on food after visiting the open-gutter latrines. She is appalled.

The children, most of them school age but with a few babies, look pale and malnourished. All of them without exception have big heads and protruding stomachs, reddish hair, and dull, dead-looking skin. A Nigerian nurse works in the camp, as well as two Nigerian ladies who travelled with the children and have been taking care of them. And then there is herself, who she believes to be their leader. Immediately after the gate stands a building with a big hall. The nurse and the two women, who also double as teachers, use the hall as their offices. Makeshift buildings make up the camp, and are used as dormitories for the children. One is equipped with windows and doors, where the women sleep.

The three women ran out to meet her when the truck dropped her inside the camp, and the driver zoomed off without waiting to introduce her to the camp keepers. The women greet her warmly. One of them, the tall black one, looks at her closely.

'Hei!' she screams. They know one another. Before the war, she and Ijeoma went to primary school together. The other ladies take her luggage into the office and give her a tour of the camp. When they show her their living quarters, she wonders where she is supposed to stay. Will it be here with them or somewhere else?

After the tour, they all return to the office, and the others wait for Ijeoma to say something. She doesn't know where to begin. Her mind whirls at what she's seen, and she questions the logic of taking these children from a war-zone to something like this. These children will all die if nothing is done to improve their living conditions.

She signs to the ladies to come close, with their chairs. They sit in a circle.

'What is the rate of mortality here?' is her first question. The nurse goes to her desk and produces a notebook in which she records all the deaths. She is about to list the names when Ijeoma stops her so that they can introduce themselves first. The nurse is Zora. Chibue is the tall, black teacher, and Adora is the fair and plump teacher.

'Thank you, all. My name is Ijeoma. I'm sorry I didn't

do this first. They sent me to take charge of the camp, but they didn't tell me that there are people here already doing so.' She scratches her head. They smile ruefully, looking at each other. She can totally understand that gesture

'Please, Chibue, can you take notes for us. I want this to be recorded as our first meeting.' Happily, Chibue goes to her desk, gets a notebook and pen, and returns, ready to take notes.

'So, Zora… the mortality…'

'Yes, Ma…'

'No, Zora: Ijeoma, please.'

'Okay. We first got here two months ago at night. Four kids died the next morning. Since then, sometimes we lose one a day, until two weeks ago when we lost only two kids in one week.'

'Excuse me, please.' Chibue says with raised hand. 'The mortality reduced since we made that gutter latrine you saw at the back of the dining hall.'

'Zora, is there any plan for covering that gutter latrine?'

'I have made a requisition for that, but no reply yet.'

'Chibue and Adora, you say you teach the kids. Can you tell me a little about what you do.' Chibue and Adora exchange glances.

'It is like this…' Chibue says. 'When we got here, we had nothing, no books, nothing, and so the three of us contributed money, the little we had, and bought exercise books and pencils. We took a flat board that we found in the yard, and scraped and polished it to use as a blackboard, only it is not black, but brown. We got chalk, and got the children together every morning and taught them. We wanted them to get the feel of being in a normal school, and they are learning.'

'My word,' Ijeoma says, and takes note. Together, they

compile all that the children and the teachers will need to have a semblance of a school.

That evening, the army van returns to take Ijeoma to where she will stay. They take her to a small but clean hostel, with running water, a bathroom, and a toilet. She thanks God for His mercies. She'd been afraid she might have to stay at the camp, but she is sorry that the others are staying there. Someone has to stay with the kids, she supposes.

The next few days, they work hard to place the children into two age-appropriate classes, with each of the two teachers minding a class. The nurse is left to take care of the medical aspect of the camp. Ijeoma spends all her spare time lobbying for the materials needed at the camp, as well as to request for the gutter latrine to be covered. She is relentless in making her requests. In the end, she is promised a shipment of the books and materials they need.

One morning, the Reverend Father who usually says Mass for them on Sundays, arrives with two huge boxes full of books. They all gather. The children jump and dance, happy to get their books at last. They open the first box and go through it, expecting to see readers, exercise books, and things like that. To their disappointment, all the box contains is Bibles.

Okay, maybe the next one has the books, but once again, the second one is full of Bibles. Ijeoma straightens up and looks the Reverend Father in the face, wanting to know the meaning behind the Bibles. He calmly and strongly says, 'These kids need the Bible now more than books. You should be teaching them the word of God and nothing more.'

The other ladies sit there looking forlorn and defeated.

Ijeoma is livid. She lashes out at the Father, and curses him out so badly that he abandons the boxes and leaves in a hurry.

That same night, two Biafran ladies, accompanied by two military personnel, pay Ijeoma a visit. They walk into her hostel room, and without speaking to her, one of the ladies goes over to the wardrobe and packs her things: clothes, shoes, everything, into her travelling bag. They lead her to the car they came in, and drive off. She suspects it must be because of her altercation with the priest that morning. She resigns herself and says nothing.

They drive her to the airport and put her on the plane to London. At the airport, one of the ladies takes her aside to brief her. 'Late this morning, the Ivorian Head of State summoned the General on your behalf. He learned that you assaulted a Reverend Father, a priest of God, and he was told to remove you at once, or you will be summarily dealt with. The General decided that the best thing is for you to leave the country. You will be met at Heathrow Airport in London and will be taken to a safe place. This is all I am allowed to tell you for now. You will get more details later in London. Safe journey.' The woman hands Ijeoma her travel papers.

In her mind, she thanks God that they are not sending her to the firing squad. Mutely, she climbs the ramp into the plane. She doesn't look back, so doesn't know whether her escorts wait to see her leave. She huddles into her seat, and her whole body shakes with foreboding, then relief when it dawns on her that God has again intervened in saving her. She is leaving all the horrors she has seen.

They arrive at Heathrow early the next morning, and she walks through the receiving hall, not so full, and sees some people holding placards. There is no indication that she is expected. She walks over to a seat, and sits to wait and take a good look round. This isn't her first time at Heathrow Airport. She has an uncle in London, and has visited him a couple of times. After waiting a few hours, she decides to call her uncle. She doesn't have his phone number, though, but she can remember his address – except for the house number. Gingerly, she goes to a phone booth and searches through the Telephone Directory. Nothing. She goes back to her seat, sits, and thinks. She sees a policeman. For so long she has been in control, weaving herself in and out of danger, helping others – now she has to let go – putting herself in the hands of others. She goes to meet the policeman.

'Sir, I think I am lost.'

'Are you from here?'

'No, Sir. I came in this morning from the Ivory Coast.'

'Blimey. Please, follow me.'

She follows him to the Police Post, and he questions her about everything under the sky. Ijeoma is careful to omit telling him that she was deported from the Ivory Coast. All they know is that she is a Biafran refugee running from the war. They decide that their best bet is to find her uncle.

Around twelve noon, her uncle, her dearest uncle, walks into the airport police office, looking worried and apprehensive. He doesn't know what to think.

'Ije,' he says with joy, and gathers her into a warm and tight embrace. 'How come? What happened?' He holds her protectively as if to shield her from the policemen.

'It is a long story, Uncle.'

The officers, in the meantime, delighted to have solved her problem, are happy to release her into the care of her uncle. She is grateful. Ijeoma thanks them, and leaves with her uncle Josh. Happy at how much she did in helping to get others to safety – now that she too, has needed such refuge. She lives to fight another day.

Resolve

Jo stepped off the train and held the package close to her side – to think that half a pound of butter and the same of tea could seem so precious! And two rashers of bacon – it was how long since she had last tasted bacon? Where her sister had got them from she didn't know. Some said that Sheffield was worse than elsewhere and that other towns hadn't had to face the shame of queuing. Now, when word went round that a particular shop had tea or butter or margarine, soap even, queues would form and people would join in passing, just on the off chance that they would pick something up. People were known to be hoarding food – those up in Broomhall with their carriages and servants weren't standing in queues, that was for sure!

Across the top of the newspaper she had been reading on the train journey down from Penistone it said: "2 million German troops massed along the Western Front." Everything was now in the balance. The Russians had quit; the Americans had at last woken up to the wickedness – the evil at the heart of Europe that would not stop and would spread and spread until it was crushed, stamped out for good. It was as Mr George said: Germany had to be delivered the knockout blow – peace could not now come without teaching them a lesson – they must be made to pay for every one of those deaths they had inflicted on the world, for every drop of blood spilt in stopping this evil.

She halted in her tracks and dropped the package – a soldier – just the way he moved – something in the way he held himself. It was here – right here – two years to the day almost. Sid had come, her childhood sweetheart, smiling, out of a crowd of his pals, holding out his arms for her, mistletoe in his cap like all the others. So many Christmases she would have to face without him – and now without her James. She had begged him not to go, he could do his bit here, doing vital work, he was so young, but in the end she knew he would have to follow his own course. After that September night – the things he'd seen that night – like so many. She had been up late knitting socks, unable to sleep until James came home. A strange noise distracted her from her stitches and she went through to the scullery for a glass of water. Out of the window she saw a dark object across the sky, going over the cemetery – a huge, long, dark cigar shape, making a strange booming noise. She had heard of Zeppelins but the actual sight of one was more terrifying than anything she had imagined. From down the cellar she heard the bombs falling as she prayed for James, and for God to intervene. James came home later, grimy and covered in dust, the air blue with his words, "Those fucking Germans – murdering children and women, and old folks! I'm going to have to go now mother." She knew then that it was settled. He was too like Sid – too like her. He had to follow his heart. She too would have picked up a bayonet and gone to Flanders if she were able.

She cursed her foolishness and picked up the brown paper bundle.

As she emerged onto the station approach the snow was starting to settle; thick heavy flakes; to make everything look pure. It even stilled the air. Was snow falling along the front too? A battlefield turned white and clean? If there were a God, would he not do the same? Pour down purity from heaven – cleanse men's souls, let them see their folly? She looked up to the sky as the dizzying flakes fell onto her and caught on her lashes. Some said this was

God's test – that the world was undergoing an ordeal of purification, she had read it somewhere: a crucible in a divine laboratory – awaiting men's minds and souls to be receptive to a transformation of humanity.

Two million Germans. She shuddered and drew her coat tighter. And yet it was on the same page that an advert for Roberts Brothers declared that fur coats were on sale for forty guineas! People, ordinary people, were tightening their belts and their resolve, working hard to save their country – laying down their lives – and some people thought it acceptable to spend forty guineas on a coat. She had scrimped and saved and gone without for that five pound war bond. She had proudly waved it as she emerged from the tank bank in Fitzalan Square. A thousand more like her and that bought one more tank like that to send over to crush the Kaiser. No wonder there were strikes. Of course it was shameful to demand more money right now, but who was it that was making all the sacrifices in this war? Ordinary people, working men and boys – whilst some were sitting on ever growing piles of gold, intending to carry on exactly as before once the war ended – if it ended – she couldn't even begin to hope. But if – or when – then there must be victory for the people. Not for Governments or the bosses. Things had got to change – wealth be spread out, power shared. Women given their rightful place. They had proved their worth: keeping the trams running, doubling productivity in her own factory over what the men used to achieve before. She looked at her hands – her broken nails and stubborn traces of black in the cracks, the hard skin on her fingers, the cuts from swarf. But it was worth it. It was her only existence. The rattle and whir of the overhead machinery, the belts racing, the cutting oil flying everywhere, the din as the lathe turned, the singing of the metal as she stripped its skin and made it shine: 9.2 inch food for a howitzer.

She slipped a little as she made her way down to the bottom of the slope. It was a good job she had cut short her visit, this snow was not giving up. She had done the right thing to pay her Christmas visit early: as they said you should avoid travelling at Christmas to free the trains for the boys. It had only been a fleeting visit, but enough to take presents for Agnes' kids, to spend a night with them – a bitter-sweet visit. Their faces so innocent, so unaware of what it was really like, this world they were to inherit. It had to be finished for their sakes so that they would never know anything like this ever again.

'Why are you crying Aunty Josephine?' they had said.

'Oh, I'm just happy to see you,' she had replied.

The Christmas party at the works: that little girl! The children had hooted and squealed at the Punch and Judy, their faces lit up at the conjuror: like it was still peacetime. She had tried to smile for them, to make things seem normal. She had helped Father Christmas – Herbert from the threading shop – to hand out the presents from under the tree. The presents they had stayed behind after their shifts to make up – for the wounded soldiers as well as the kids. The little girl – she had tugged on Father Christmas' red coat. He had turned round to see the little mite staring up at him with her big eyes. He had stooped and said: 'Have you been a good girl?' She had nodded shyly.

'And what would you like for Christmas?'

'Father Christmas, will you please bring my Daddy back?'

'I will try my hardest sweetheart,' Herbert had replied. She had put down the pile of presents she was holding for

Herbert and got out of the canteen in a hurry.

As soon as she was home she would put the kettle on, get out her needles and see how many more she could add to that pile of facecloths she was knitting for the boys. Then an early start in the morning.

Another day at the works turning shells for killing other mother's sons.

Bluebell Memories

Jo stepped off the train and held the package close to her side. The station's clock struck ten. Her journey down from London had provided ample opportunity to plan the day ahead. Before handing over the keys and paper work, she'd carry out a final check of her grandfather's house, from the attic to the garden shed. As she walked along the platform screeching gulls welcomed her return, and the bracing sea air brought salt to her lips – reminiscent of her childhood visits.

Jo had loved coming down to spend the school holidays with her grandfather in this part of Kent, and she'd continued to visit him throughout her university years. There had always been so much to see and do as a child. Today was her first visit to Folkestone since his funeral. Jo took out the keys, hesitated for a moment, and then opened the front door.

The warm welcome she'd always received was no longer there. The house was just that – a house, no longer the home of her beloved grandfather. Most of the furniture had already been sold and what little was left she'd include within the auction sale. Reckoning that it would only take a couple of hours at the most, she pulled down the ladder, climbed into the loft and switched on the torch.

Ducking beneath the wooden rafters, she gingerly edged her way towards the chimney breast at the far end, taking care to avoid standing on the more exposed areas, where thick glass fibre insulation was the only thing between her and the bedroom ceilings. It felt as cold up there as it had been standing by her grandfather's grave. She shivered and illogically looked over her shoulder to see if she'd been followed. There was no-one, of course. The space was as empty as she felt, but she still breathed a sigh of relief.

As Jo turned back, she almost lost her balance but quickly managed to grab onto a large beam to right herself. It was then that she noticed something wedged between two joists.

It was a small Peek Frean's biscuit tin. Prising open the rusted lid she was disappointed to see that there was nothing but a stained rag inside. Intrigued as to why it was there, she nipped the hessian and lifted it out. A small, tan-coloured notebook fell onto the loft insulation.

Golden letters were carved out on the front: AWH. Her interest was piqued – they were her grandfather's initials. Five minutes later she had clambered back down the ladder and was standing in front of the kitchen window, the final house-check temporarily forgotten.

With the tip of her index fingers Jo traced the name. Written in faded ink on the inside front cover were the words *Albert William Hurd (aged 12 years)*. She pressed the leather book against her nose. It smelt musty. The dankness had claimed some of the pages over the years, forever concealing the secrets of a young boy. The remaining pages crinkled as she flicked through the book. Around the middle, pressed against the spine, she discovered a faded flower – a bluebell. Was it a marker for an important entry, she wondered? She jumped up onto the laminate worktop, settled herself, and then looked at the date. It was written almost eighty years ago.

She dithered. Should she read on? Her grandfather had never talked much about his youth and had certainly never spoken about either of the wars, no matter how much her younger brother had pestered him for information.

'Did you shoot anyone, Gramps?' Michael had asked.

'How could I? I was only nine when the First World War broke out. Thirteen when it ended.'

Michael had pressed on, oblivious to his grandfather's irritation. 'But, you must have seen soldiers and bombs and blood and Germans in the second one?'

'I do remember me Dad in uniform, when he left for the front line during the Great War. And I remember me Mam's tears, when he didn't return,' their grandfather had replied.

Jo's six-year-old brother had uncharacteristically paused, albeit briefly, before moving onto his next question.

'Did your Dad shoot any Germans then, Gramps?'

That was when Jo had offered to take Michael to the park. She'd been aware, even then, that this barrage of questions was upsetting their grandfather. He never did tell them anything more about his war years, apart from the fact that he was a police officer during the Second World War.

Feeling like an interloper, Jo studied the cursive script of her grandfather's younger hand, so carefully presented on the diary's pages.

"Friday, 25th May 1917

A warm and sunny day, one I'll never forget for as long as I live.
On me way to school I saw Mr Stokes who asked if I'd help Ernest with the deliveries later that afternoon, being as it was Bank Holiday weekend and all that. I jumped at the chance, especially as he'd offered me a farthing and some vegetables, which I thought would be a nice birthday present for me Mam.

Never did get me farthing and veg… but at least I'm still alive. I started at 4pm. It was still hot and I hoped to get the deliveries done quickly so that I could join me mates for a game of football before tea. It took me over two hours because of the bombing. The air raid came from nowhere. I found shelter in the outhouse of one of our customers on Bournemouth Road. When I eventually got back to Tontine Street, the shop had disappeared. Direct hit. I wasn't allowed to go anywhere near Stokes' so I turned the bike round and headed back home. That was when I saw our neighbour's baby.

At first, I couldn't see much because of the smoke. It looked like someone had left a football on the step of what was Playfair's Shoe Shop, and I went to pick it up. That was how I discovered her body beneath all the dust and rubble. I just managed to turn away before throwing up. Her eyes, once the colour of bluebells, were now dull and lifeless. It was Flo, our neighbour's baby, and she was dead. I'll never forget those eyes. She was staring up at me, begging for help.

I didn't want her big sister to see her like that so I took me school jumper off and covered her. I hope it had been a quick death and that she hadn't cried for long.

How I hate the Boche! I hope the warden finds her soon.

Mam was crying when I got back. She thought I'd copped it.

Saturday, 26ᵗʰ May 1917

I didn't sleep at all last night. I kept hearing the moans and groans of the injured. I could even smell the blood and burning of buildings and bodies. Every time I closed me eyes I saw Baby Flo. This morning Mam told me that all of next door had been out shopping on Tontine Street when the silver birds of death visited. Not one of our neighbours is alive!

I couldn't tell her about baby Flo, even when she clipped me round the ear for losing me jumper.

Sunday, 27ᵗʰ May, 1917

It's Mam's birthday. She loved the bluebells I picked for her. I also took some back to the bombsite..."

Jo closed the diary, marking the page with the birthday flower and wiped away the tears that had pooled beneath her spectacles. She knew now why her grandfather hadn't shared his memories of war – he had wanted to protect her and Michael from the horror of his nightmares.

Closing the gate behind her for the last time, she caught her first glimpse of spring beneath the ornamental cherry tree in the centre of the front lawn, and smiled.

Bluebells. Her favourite.

Cogs

Joe stepped off the train and held the package close to his side. 'This way, Sir.' Still strange how in his own mind he was Joe – what his mother used to call him – and yet to the wider world he was "Sir." Even to his wife Florence he was Joseph.

'Your car to take you to Whitehall, Sir.' The voice linked to an outstretched arm guided him towards the pre-cleared exit and the Lanchester, warm and inviting. The weather was fierce: biting winds turning the drizzle to driving icicles. Sir Joseph Harrison MP gave a sideways glance towards the group of women and small children huddled outside the station, no shelter from this icy blast, realising they had been held there so he could pass through unhindered.

A balding, red-faced fat man. That's how he was portrayed in the newspaper cartoons. That's what he was, what he had become. Privileged in probably all of the ways it was possible to be privileged, the well-fed, plump, rosy-cheeked complexion had always accompanied his ramrod posture and perfect English accent. A red-faced fat man. Too important to be held up for a second on his journey from the full English breakfast in his comfortable train cabin to the comfort of the leather seats of the car parked snugly against the kerb of the cobbled station approach.

As the car pulled away, he turned his attention to the manila folder in his hand. The "Top Secret" printed in explosive red capitals on the front of every such folder, that once gave him a small thrill, now induced dread. He pulled his reluctant attention to the memo in front of him but recoiled at the enormity of the decision he was forced to make. Once confident, reliant on his English stiff upper lip, he had lately doubted he had the stomach, the bravery or whatever it was that was needed for this: the dropping of thousands of tons of explosives over a city which was home to the kind of ordinary people he saw out of the window as his car rolled by. And yet, if it hastened surrender it would save countless more lives, so the argument went, but it did little to ease the heaviness weighing on his chest.

No-nonsense parenting and public school had taught him to be a practical man not an emotional one, and now his country required it. But he was getting old and tired. He had begun to resent facing them day in day out: looking to him for answers, trusting him with the lives of their loved ones. He knew it was the snapshots he captured now, the seemingly unimportant, fleeting, everyday scenes that would stay with him, that would recreate themselves so starkly in the half light of early morning as he berated his body, his soul, for another sleepless night. The faces of the bewildered evacuees, the grim countenances of widows, the wounded getting on with the life remaining; refusing to be defeated, making do with pitiful rations and eking out what little resources they had. They were always silent, respectful, stoic, trusting. Of course he had no experience to draw on to feel a fraction of the exhaustion of a body shivering relentlessly from the cold, let alone the physical agony of a heart cleft by the brutal death of a son sentenced to die for his country. He admired them but they provoked in him a deep shame and anger that could be hard to bear and hard to shake off.

What would be the use of him trying to do anything different? Insisting he be the one to wait out in the cold to let them pass? He could give away every Harris Tweed he owned, give away every pound and shilling from his trust fund, it would make little difference. The war was consuming them all one way or another. Joe doubted any amount of corpulent Old Harrovians putting together a Top Secret report, calling indulgent lunch meetings, discussing, planning and cleverly pushing little flags across the world map could make any real difference. But if he didn't make the unthinkable decisions, who would?

He rubbed his chest and tried to slow his breathing, remembering he was, for it all, just a man. A man like the thousands already dead and mutilated. Like the officers he had known, shaken hands with and clapped on the back, like the ordinary working men he'd never met and would never meet. Nothing more than circumstances had brought him to the table of the decision makers instead of the front line. He ran a clammy hand over his tired eyes and stared out again at the icy rain pelting the shiny black car. The world had never seen anything like this. How could a few, well educated men even begin to pretend this could be controlled when the daily briefings of the dead, mutilated or missing and now thousands of innocent families being murdered, had become as commonplace as hearing the weather report each morning?

No man should have such power, such responsibility. But if not him, then who? No mind could be expected to the bear the sights, sounds and reports that filled his days without some method of mental gymnastics for self-delusion and self-preservation. It took great effort, a dissociation from the mundane, from the shocking, the barbaric, at which Joe had forced himself to become all too skilled but which was starting to take its toll.

He unclenched his fists, cleared his throat and brought himself back to the memo in his hand. Yet another meeting of Commodores, Deputy Chiefs of Staff and

Chiefs of Staff, dragging him into the, just, still beating heart of the Capital of the once great Empire to play God with their fellow men.

The Lanchester drew to a stop snugly against another kerb. The door was opened and an unnecessary large black umbrella emerged. Joe caught his reflection in the shiny brass plaque of the ministry's oak doors. A balding, red-faced fat man. So precious, let not even a flake of snow fall on to his Saville Row overcoat.

With hat, overcoat and leather gloves swiftly dispatched, chit chat about an old rugby rivalry and the weather dispensed with, and a china cup of sweet tea in his hand, he cleared his throat to call the room to order.

'Gentlemen. Shall we begin? I trust all have had the briefing paper?'

Nods and murmurs of assent pressed Joe to continue: 'A swift consensus is desirable. The Prime Minister himself is waiting to be briefed at the earliest opportunity.'

Joe recalled little of the two hours that followed, less of the three course lunch, and even less following the third brandy. A consensus was reached, the orders were given, his job was done. In the midst of it all, he allowed himself the thought: in the eye of this storm, what is the alternative – and concluded there was none.

*

The flames from the fireplace reflected in the highly polished fender. This was his favourite time of day. Sat in his favourite armchair, slippers and dressing gown on. Privacy. In the private apartments, away from the housekeeper; no need for keeping up appearances. He ignored the babbling on the Home Service and the equally constant babbling from Florence, who inexplicably busied herself coming in and out of the room. He switched the wireless off before the news and padded over to his drink cabinet, and fetched his favourite briar. Here, at least, all was ordered, as it should be, and under control. A pipe and a whisky, then he would turn in and read a few more pages of *Mr Midshipman Easy* before lights out.

Florence returned and switched the wireless back on: 'It's time for War Report.'

The familiar voice entered the room:

"Allied bombers again flew over Germany… Dresden…"

As Joe scrambled to switch it off, the lead crystal glass fell and shattered.

All the Same

Joe stepped off the train and held the package close to his side. He winced as the pain receptors flared up again. Gingerly, he stepped onto platform two, the damned metal leg clinking as his foot hit the ground. He grimaced, his body still hurting from the old laser war wounds. He looked down and saw the pain receptors were glowing all sorts of blues. Of sea blue, ultramarine, sky blue, turquoise and cobalt. They flashed and danced up his leg, to his arm, and all across his torso. Where the laser bullets had shot him down. He'd need to get it seen to: if he could afford it. Ugly patches of metal where holes had been messily repaired in the field, gaping to reveal the damage beneath. Holes where the blues were reflected like diamonds. In the light of the lamps on the ceiling they danced. Even under his uniform. They twinkled like far away stars as they danced merrily towards his brain and neurons to remind him that it hurt. He rolled his eyes in annoyance. It was just typical. He was trying to get his life back to normal and he was reminded of the past by pain. He reached inside a pocket of his army kitaskin jacket. Rustling the fabric, he searched for a shiny violet pill. Balancing the package in one hand, he clumsily inserted the pill into his brain, shutting the pain off for a while.

As he stepped forward onto the platform, he was hit by the crowd. Like the waves of the sea, they drowned and absorbed him. They clustered round him. Their loud voices and bodies, so close, made him claustrophobic. Suddenly there was no light, no air above. Enclosed. Trapped. No escape. It was so tight he could feel people breathing down the back of his neck. He couldn't take it. It was too small. His mind began to conjure all sorts of scenarios. Of small spaces and prison cells. Prison cells he had rescued people from on Jaskla. Prison cells with rotting slave corpses that wanted him to stay. Shuddering, he blinked the nightmares away. Panicking at the lack of space, he wanted to bolt. He was shaking all over. To his relief, the crowd broke way. He breathed as he saw light again through the gap of people and walked towards it. With legs that trembled as if they had been rocked by an earthquake. Not looking where he was going, he was jostled by a family of Glastre people. Refugees. Ones the Zakla Rebellion had always liked to shoot and experiment on for their crystal skins. Innocent civilians. Each vividly coloured face turned to apologetic smiles, stammering out sorry in their single bleeps and bloops. He smiled back. He muttered that it didn't matter. The package had been knocked out of his hand as they had bumped into him. The tallest, and the oldest of the group, with a shiny vermilion crystal coloured face, leaned down to pick it up. His limbs wobbled as he made them malleable. Skin and crystals melted as he knelt. The amethyst and scarlet tints to his crystal skin rippled as he bent down. Reflecting his organs beneath. Light from lamps on the ceiling made streaks of reflections dance off him, like a rainbow. Melting his hand into another shape to pick the package up, he rose slowly with it. Holding it delicately, careful not to bend it, he gave it back to Joe. Joe thanked him, and went on his way as they stepped onto the hyperspace train. He carefully checked that none of his papers had fallen out. He couldn't lose them. They were important. The report of what he had faced in the years, with his own papers and journal from the neuron chips of what he had seen. He flicked through it all, checking nothing had been lost. Luckily, nothing had fallen out. Heaving a sigh of relief, he collected himself and walked towards the exit.

Apart from being hit by that small family, he was hit by all sorts of feelings. It was just so.......strange. That was the word. But, yet, not quite the word. The war had taken him from home for years. For him, everything had changed completely. And yet, here was the old Letchworth Garden City station. Exactly as it had been. The same. The same rush of people who were hurrying to London Kings Cross on the hyperspace train for home after work. The same cluster around the pillars where the train times were displayed. Close to it, the same bright green robot who announced everything. With his whistle that always came out from his stomach with its piercing cry when the train came. There was even that same jolly robot by the coffee shop who had been there for as long as Joe could remember. He was in his usual brightly coloured, amber and violet metallic skin, trying to sell the neuron chip of this week's newspaper to anyone who would buy one. Or today's news broadcast on Hina Station Two. They were all muddled up in his large scarlet cardboard box, just as usual. The robots made him angry. He had fought against them for years. Robots who had bombed and killed. Just because they believed they were better. Across the planets. He had been shot by them. On multiple occasions. He had a minefield of metal holes in him to prove it. But now here they were in society, being all polite. Being helpful. It made the fury rise in his stomach. It bubbled and boiled. At the thought that they could even consider being a part of society after everything the Zakla Rebellion had done. His clenched fists shook in anger as he passed the robot. He put the anger to one side. It was hard, but he tried. He couldn't start a riot. Not here. It would make matters worse. Besides, these robots probably didn't even know what their kind had done. He walked across the station, holding the package tightly and looked round. But it was all the same. Nothing had changed, despite their victory. Despite the hundreds and thousands of lives lost, of Joe's friends, of civilians. People went on with their lives just as they had done. As if it didn't matter to them. And that was the saddest part – that they didn't even acknowledge it. He didn't understand it. How could they forget? He couldn't forget. Never. He didn't want to. Except to avoid the nightmares. But he couldn't forget the sacrifice. He couldn't forget the thousands of grateful, liberated people. He couldn't forget seeing his own friends die in front of his eyes. In the name of these people. It made him question if it had been worth it. Or, like most wars, it didn't matter.

The same benches for people long gone. Their plaques which glittered in honour although they were ignored and forgotten. And beside it, a small statue of a soldier with a laser gun. He stared out, with glazed eyes, at a fixed point only he saw. He looked proud, as if he alone stood for all the soldiers and their honour. At his feet, by the grimy and heavy boots, it read: In Memory of Soldiers in the Zaklan War. Underneath this sign, the dates printed in smaller letters hit Joe with reality. It made him realise just how long he'd been away. He wondered who was King now, who was President now. He wondered what currency was in now, or what fashion was new this season. What sestball team was winning, or what new pub was open. And his friends who wouldn't be there to see it all. Their favourite chair in the pub left empty. Their favourite pint not ordered. It made him realise how much he'd missed. And who he would miss. And how much he would miss them. It overwhelmed him. How he could have been one of them. Buried and forgotten. To be just a plaque. Joe wiped away a small tear as he remembered thousands who would be just that. Just a name on a bench. When they had been so much more. They had had lives and loves and families. But they had been wiped out without a care. As the universe believed they didn't matter. But they had mattered.

There was a small donation box for soldiers by the side of the statue. Rummaging in his pockets, he found a few small coins. With fumbling fingers, he posted them in the grateful slot. In honour, he made a small salute to the bench and its small memorial. Swallowing the rest of his tears, he walked on his way. No one looked round at him. But he looked round at them. Observing how it was all so disturbingly similar. It was just as he remembered it. They were all too absorbed in their daily lives. Just as Joe remembered. Groups of Enzak people sat on the benches talking and sipping their coffees through their long tongues that connected to the drinks like straws. Human neighbours on the bench had a glazed look, taking today's news on the neuron chips that the robot sold. The same small coffee shop by the exit. The same crowds. That ignored the coffee shop. The same eagerness of the crowd to get to the exit. Through the portal door, direct to their homes. The same way they shifted impatiently on either foot. How they jiggled. How they craned aching necks to see how long the queue would be. And as usual, complaining to their neighbour in the queue. The coffee shop that was lit up the same as a result of flashes of sunset orange energy in the portal attacking its humble emerald painted walls. As they stepped through the portal. The sunset orange flashes bounced, like usual, reflected on the same sapphire robot nearby that swiped the tickets emblazoned on the passengers' arms. Like always, he said "Have A Nice Day" in that same cheerful tone. Even if no one ever said it back. The same tablet outside, displaying what coffee and muffin was today's special in bright letters on the screen. It was risklaberry muffins today. He smiled. They had always been his favourite. It made him think of home. Of life before the army. When his grandmother had her bakery beneath their house and always made her delicious cakes and muffins. Of spare muffins on a Sunday, that wanted tasting for Monday. That smell made so many memories come to mind. He wondered if they were still there. They probably were. He imagined his grandfather being so surprised as he showed up, so proud of Joe. The comforting hugs that asked if he was okay but understood that he wasn't really. Of his grandmother making extra muffins especially for his visit. He smiled at the sweet memories.

He walked towards the coffee shop, the package held tightly in his hand. The door opened with its small musical ding! As the door opened, the gorgeous smell of the ripe risklaberries and sweet chocolate over the top wafted out. Of the heavenly bitter but sweet scent of coffees that wafted out alongside them. He decided to get one. Well, he did deserve one. And there was time before he had to meet Commander Blagrac. Boots clacked against the albino white marble floor as he walked. They were as loud as laser gunshots. Cutting chunks in the atmosphere. Everyone turned round to stare at him as he walked in his uniform. The footsteps scared him a little. He thought they were some robot that was marching along to shoot him down. But they weren't. He looked around jerkily, just in case. But they weren't. The people seemed to gaze at him in awe, or was it pity, or disgust, or shame? As if they didn't want to be shaken from their insularity, to be reminded of the brutality that had reigned for so long out there. Their wide eyed stares were hard to miss. He had just done his duty. Because it was the right thing to do. All he wanted was that people try to understand. To stop it happening ever again. One elderly gentleman with three kindly green eyes tipped his straw coloured hat to Joe. Joe nodded. But he kept walking, not wanting to draw any more attention to himself. The boots echoed behind him. And with them was the war. The memories of marching over countless such foreign terrains on some mission or another. It rushed before his eyes for a minute. He blinked the vision away hastily .

It was all the same. But for Joe, it couldn't be any less similar. The similar had been made alien for Joe. Everything had changed. It was like he was in a dream. As if everything he had seen and done in the war hadn't happened. As if he had woken up from some nightmare and back into his old life. Back into reality. It was petrifying. More unnerving than all the monsters he had faced. Even more harrowing than all the insane robots in the entire Zakla Rebellion. To not know where he stood anymore. It was a relief for the war to be over. For that call to go home to be heard. As it was shouted out with exuberance across the trenches of muddy Amslak. They had known it would end sometime. Nothing ever lasts forever. But now it had ended. Now it was over. And he had been thrown back into his old life. and he had no idea where to start. He had his orders to report back to the Flidax Station For Soldiers in Letchworth, and to deliver the package to Commander Blagrac. But after that, he just didn't know. It would be so different. In the war, he had known what to do. He had been on the front line. Fighting insane robots every day. Running across the bare war zones to fire the laser bullets. Bullets that embedded themselves in the next line of the machine army with their explosions of coloured light. He even still smelt slightly of the electric gunpowder. Of dust and blood and dirt that the war came with, bringing him back to it with its pungent smell.

That life had become normal. But now, he had no idea. He felt lost. Bewildered. As if he was one of the refugees on a new planet, far away. Lost from family and friends. Lost from his own identity. Lost from everything but still alive. It was terrifying. An all soul consuming feeling. As if he was one of the slave robots he had seen on countless planets, stripped of everything except the empty shell. Made to march on because they were ordered to. He even felt robotic as he put his feelings aside and attempted to put one foot in front of the other. As he tried to carry on. Even though he knew his feelings wouldn't be suppressed. That the tears and rage were bubbling away under the mask he put on to hide it all. Perplexed, he wondered how the other soldiers did it. How they carried on with their lives after war. After facing countless odds, horrors and deaths and then being thrown back to normality. He shook his head in confusion. He didn't understand how to do it. It was just all so.......strange.

Nintendo Warrior

Joe stepped off the train and held the package close to his side as if the attention of everyone at the station was on it. Forcing normality, he pulled up the collar and hood of his coat to hide the bruises and cuts on his face. He paused to buy a newspaper headlined, "Pullman Drone Strike Assassination?" before walking out of the station. He paused on the sidewalk, looked around him and then read the sub-heading. "Who is Steering the War Machine?"

A smiling, kind-faced grandfather with gaudy election-victory confetti in his wispy white hair stared up at Joe from the front page. He stuffed the newspaper into a bin and walked on.

'Welcome to Holloman Airforce Base, Alamogordo. Here recruits train to be 18Xs – the best remotely-piloted aircraft operators in the world.

'Your weapons of choice: the MQ-1F Predator, armed with two AGM-116 Hellfire missiles and a bunch of cameras, sensors and all shit like that and, the star of the show, the MQ-9D Reaper, armed with GBU-17 Paveway IV laser-guided bombs, AGM-119 Hellfire III air-to-ground missiles, AIM-903 Sidewinders, GBU-58 Joint Direct Attack Munitions and AIM-100 Stinger air-to-air missiles.

'Make no mistake, these aircraft are lethal. They kill people. This is what you signed up for and this is the reality. As a serving 18X, you will be expected to pull the trigger on command.

'And you will pull that trigger, son, because taking out just one terrorist can save dozens, hundreds, maybe

even thousands of innocent lives – and your hesitation might cost just as many.'

The walk home took longer than usual. Joe followed a circuitous route, taking a long-cut through the park and stopping often to rest his swollen knee, forever glancing at the people behind and around him, searching their faces. He scanned the featureless overcast sky constantly, brow furrowed and wet.

The breeze ruffled suburban leaves and flags just as it always did. A child hurtled along on a rattling bike, head down, fascinated by the front wheel going round. Petra drove past in her new umpteenth-hand Ford, throwing him a wave and one of her smiles. He waved back quickly to keep his hand off the package for as short a time as possible.

It's confirmed. That is the target to the left of the camel. You ready for this, son?'

'I am, Sir.'

'Take your time. He can't see you and there's not a lot of cover so you can afford to wait until he's relatively clear of his friends. Looks like he's arguing with them, waving his arms about. If you give it a minute he might storm off or something, then you can nail him clean.'

'Yes, Sir. I'm in a standard stealth holding pattern at eleven thousand feet.'

'Good. Okay, they're shaking hands. Get ready.'

'Package armed and locked on target, Sir.'

'Fire.'

'Package away. Target lock steady.'

'Look at the bastard. He doesn't have a clue what's coming.'

'C... Contact. Target eliminated, Sir. Jesus Christ.'

'It's good to feel bad, son, but never forget that these bastards are the enemy.'

'No, Sir. I'm sorry, Sir, it won't happen again.'

'Good. Take five, go grab a coffee or something.'

Joe kicked a path through empty pizza boxes and beer bottles towards his desk. He set the package down and then switched on his Frankensteined computer. While he waited for it to boot, he picked up the package and opened it with bruised and trembling hands. Inside was a computer hard drive bearing the legend, "Property of the U.S. Air Force/C.I.A. Liaison Office" and an official seal. He turned the hard drive over in his hands, probed the stitches in his lip with his tongue.

He took a deep breath and then ripped the seal.

'Sir, I think... I think there were children in those trucks... women... Oh shit.'

'Keep it together. If al-Zawahiri chose to shield himself with innocents, that's on his own soul. By taking him out, you've done a great service for peace and stability in the Middle East and the world. A little collateral damage to get that bastard is well worth it. You think scum like al-Zawahiri worried about women and kids on nine-eleven, son?'

'No, Sir, of course not. It's just...'

'Come on, pilot, spit it out.'

'We've supposedly taken al-Zawahiri out three times now, Sir. How do we know...'

'You don't get paid to know, you get paid to do. Now, watch your fuel. One more scan-pass then r.t.b.'

'Yes, Sir.'

'You're doing fine, son. Better than fine. Keep it up. There's a big project in the pipe and I want you on it, so don't screw up.'

The Frankensteined computer was ready. The stolen hard drive was ready. The internet connection, encrypted and anonymised, was ready. All that remained was to connect them. To slide the stolen drive into an external port. The simplest part of the whole plan, and the point of no return.

Joe picked his way into the kitchen and filled the kettle. Rinsed out a mug. Waited for the kettle to boil, sucking his grazed knuckles. He looked through the open kitchen door towards the patient computer and then down at the untidy floor. He nudged an empty Bud bottle with his toe, rolling it to clink against another, and sighed. Joe opened the door under the sink and pulled out two trash bags and then, after a pause, reached in for another two. The kettle boiled unheeded.

'We've been impressed with your performance.'

'Thank you, Sir.'

'Now. We want you for something special. Activate the console, please.'

'Booting. Logging in. Console active, Sir.'

'Select feed MQ-9s/00816.'

'That's a simulation feed, Sir.'

'Not tonight it's not. Select the feed, please.'

'Loading. Sir... Sir, this bird's in the United States.'

'I know where it is. Here's your target data and

satellite links.'

'I've never seen tech like this before, Sir. The detail is fantastic.'

'Well, you're in the Big Leagues now, son. Get used to it.'

'Target located – Sir, is this right?'

'Target confirmed.'

'But Sir, this guy's an American citizen, in America. I've seen him on the news. I'm not sure if this is...'

'Is what? Right?'

'Yes, Sir. It just seems a... big step.'

'Follow my orders. The target is verified and authorized. Take control of the aircraft.'

'I... I have control, Sir. All systems normal.'

'Good. Proceed to target. Full stealth mode.'

Joe turned on the television and surfed to the news. True to his word, the President appeared at the appointed time. He acknowledged the applause and photo-flashes with an impatient wave and then opened a leather folder on the lectern bearing his seal. Joe plugged the hard drive into his computer. The devices synchronised and hummed to each other like shy lovers. He waited. The front door remained inert and in one piece. The lights stayed on. No sirens, flashing beacons or tyre-screeches outside. The President cleared his throat and paused, considering the weight of the situation. Joe scanned the overcast night sky through the window and frowned. He drew down the blind and then shook his head, smiling at the folly.

'My fellow Americans, and our friends and allies throughout the world, good evening. I have a short statement, after which I will not be taking questions but the Assistant Press Secretary will be available for that purpose. It is now unfortunately clear that the death last week of my good friend and loyal colleague, Senator James Pullman, was murder. More than this, it was murder committed with United States military hardware. Even more troubling, in these already troubled times, is that this strike came from deep within the over-complex systems and intricate hierarchies of our own military structure. This country faces a danger which cannot be ignored, a possible military coup. But, in perceiving this nebulous plot, I have only delayed it. I must act quickly and decisively in order to destroy this imminent threat to our freedoms, liberties and way of life. Twenty minutes ago, with a heavy heart, I signed an Executive Order postponing the current elections until the crisis is past. I shall remain as president, with the full support of Congress and the Judiciary, and with the safety of our continent, indeed the safety of our planet, at heart. I call upon all loyal Americans - whether in uniform or not, at home or abroad - stand with me now in the cause of freedom and do not suffer these military tyrants to rise. That is all I have to say for the time being. Please excuse me, I have a lot to do. Goodnight, and God bless America.'

> *'Well, well, well, what do we have here?'*
> *'I'm an RPA operator.'*
> *'Fucking toys. You geeks aren't allowed in here – this bar's for real pilots, not cowards who shoot people from half-way around the world.'*
> > *'I just want to drink my drink in peace, okay?'*
> > *'Say "sir" when addressing a superior, geek.'*
> > *'We're the same rank.'*
> > *'Like Hell. You're only an imaginary soldier, a*

momma's boy Nintendo Warrior. You get shot down, you just get a "Game Over" and pick another toy without getting off your spotty fat asses. We get shot down, we're fucked. Wouldn't catch me hiding behind a computer when there's man's work to be done.'

'Hiding? You know, I see everyone I kill. I see them in real time. I see them torn apart and I watch them get blasted into mist. I watch their trucks turn to confetti and their houses explode and burn. I watch their blood, emulsion white in the infra red, squirting out of them. I watch survivors dragging themselves away, squirting white, leaving trails of white, then falling still and going dark. I see what I've done. You cowboys just pop a missile fifty miles out then turn around and run home without seeing squat. You're the ones hiding.'

'I'm going to kick your ass for that, you pathetic nerd.'

"LOG IN TO 18X SECURE SERVER?" Joe clicked the Yes button and opened an encrypted virtual terminal through a TOR browser. Assuming they weren't onto him already, and if anyone noticed and bothered to look, they'd think he was connecting from a server in Washington D.C. A smile danced across his face and then he set his jaw and jacked into the network. It was busy, far busier than he'd ever seen it. He took a swig of beer, stinging the stitched split in his lip. The abandoned kettle clicked as it cooled. Three full trash bags rustled by the door as their contents settled. He browsed the list of active missions in United States airspace and found every single unit in use. He steepled his fingers, regarding the screen for a long moment, and then reached for the mouse.

'Time to rock and roll.'

'What the Hell were you thinking? You know that place is full of Air Force pilots, at least you should do by now. You're one of my best operators, yet you go and make a rookie mistake like this. I expect more of you. I thought you were smart?'

'I felt I deserved their respect, Sir.'

'Respect? By getting yourself beaten to a pulp by some cocky-assed fly-boy?'

'No, Sir. I thought I could make them understand, that's all. Understand that what we do is important and valid. We keep them from dangerous jobs, we provide cover when they're on-mission, we supply accurate data to their mission-planners and commanders.'

'And kill people.'

'Sir, I wasn't boasting about that. I just... I'm sorry, Sir, I really don't know why I said that.'

'Be that as it may, this is very frustrating. You know what's happening tonight?'

'Operation Freedom's Beacon, Sir, the nationwide readiness exercise.'

'And I wanted you on my Omega Team as leader.'

'Thank you, Sir. I'd be honoured...'

'Stow it. That little scrap's blown it for you. You're suspended pending psychiatric investigation. I am extremely disappointed in you, pilot. Collect your gear and get off this base until I send for you, is that clear?'

'Yes Sir. I really am sorry, Sir.'

'Dismissed.'

Of the fifteen hundred drones operating in U.S. airspace, a thousand had specific targets. The rest were configured for distraction and support. The targets were senators, judges, military personnel, journalists, public officials, celebrities, businesspeople, scientists, writers, artists, bloggers. The list was endless. Tracking feeds showed most of these targets being drawn into small groups under the pretence of emergencies, or events and gatherings arranged months in advance. Some were running late and assigned to support drones. The President, aboard Air Force One and escorted by sixteen manned fighter jets as he made his way to the newly opened Crisis Command Bunker deep beneath Mount Rushmore, was not a target.

The mass-assassination was scheduled to take place in just over two hours in the guise of, Joe suspected, an exercise hi-jacked by rogue generals conspiring with the President. He pulled down the Availability menu and selected the closest RPA to Air Force One. It was a humble reconnaissance model, unarmed, but good enough for the purpose. Time to cut the head off the snake.

'He did it?'

'Yes.'

'Is he believable?'

'One of my best; history of asking questions but one Hell of an operator. Got himself suspended to go home and stop us. Stole a jack-drive on his way out.'

'I trust that isn't going to be a problem.'

'Nope.'

'And the President?'

'In his bunker under the White House.'

'Excellent. Is Phase Two still on schedule?'

'He'll try to stop it but yes. Ten minutes.'

'He can't, can he?'

'Not a hope. We just need the C.I.A. to find his computer jacked into our system, that's all. The rest we can file under national security.'

The mid-air destruction of Air Force One following a collision with an unmanned drone which avoided the fighter escort with acrobatic ease hit the news networks almost immediately. There was even footage of the burning wreckage falling out of the sky. It was almost as if they were ready for it. The countdown to the mass-strike didn't stop with Joe's intervention. Didn't pause as he'd expected. Joe's fingers worried at the keyboard without effect until, at precisely 10:17pm, over 3,000 people were killed in 1,117 simultaneous drone strikes on domestic American targets. Sick to his stomach, Joe staggered to the window and opened the blind. The sky was nothing but a vague black void behind the street lamps' blue LED glare.

'My fellow Americans,' the President said from the television. 'At the request of the Joint Chiefs, I was not aboard Air Force One when it was brutally attacked earlier this evening. Reports are reaching us, however, that hundreds, perhaps even thousands of Americans, have not been so fortunate. This atrocity was apparently the work of one of our own drone pilots who was lured into terrorism through a misplaced sense of guilt, alcoholism and post-traumatic stress disorder. He overrode the system and turned our own drone network against us, robbing us of some of our most important and beloved Americans, and we are all the poorer for it. All I can say about him at the moment is that his name was Joe, he was an American and he was killed just a few minutes ago, preferring to turn a drone on himself rather than submit to the C.I.A. agents closing in on him. It seems inconceivable that Joe executed this attack without help. Rest assured, I will root out…'

'It's confirmed. That is the target standing at the highlighted window. You ready for this, son?'
     'I am, Sir.'

Here and now

Joe stepped off the train and held the package close to his side. Searching for leads amongst those papers had whiled away the hours from Boulogne. It was years since he had passed through Amiens, "InterRailing" as a student. It smelt like he remembered France to smell, but the new glass canopy outside the station said the town had bridged the centuries.

Sat outside a café opposite the station, he ordered a Pastis, though he couldn't quite remember whether he liked it – funny how it was a girls' drink back home – Sonia drank it with blackcurrant. He sat back and pulled some papers from the big Tyvek envelope: the copy of the birth certificate from the General Register Office – they'd had a small fortune off him; Alfred Ironside, cool name! Instead of a signature, the little cross, the 'mark' of his mother Alice. The 1911 census – his last – aged 14, butcher's boy; six people in two rooms in Bessemer Place.

He poured water from the jug into the glass, turning it creamy, and slugged back some of the sweet liquid – this was better than North Wales in the rain with Sonia.

He was proud of Alf. He spread out the hand-drawn family tree. Not branches – tendrils; reaching back into the past. So many lives that led to him, so much toil in mines and fields, foundries and workshops; and so much heartache – branches that ended in buds nipped out in infancy. All the hours he had spent on the computer, Sonia berating him for wasting £155 on his *Ancestry* "worldwide" subscription, and for not coming to bed till gone two in the morning. The frustration: those women changing their names on marrying just to thwart him, make him spend more money, scattergun, on marriage certificates trying to find maiden names. The impossible Smith branch: how could you narrow it down from 360 matches! The hours going boggle-eyed at different county archives trawling microfilms of Parish registers to little avail; trying to get back beyond the eighteenth century, trying to find a Roundhead or someone with blue blood: someone to raise him above the ordinary. He'd even settle for a notorious murderer! But it seemed he came from a boring family of farm labourers turned miners turned shop workers.

When someone found a war hero on *"Who do you think you are?"* – *"Who the hell do they think they are?"* Sonia called it – he envied them. Unfortunately, his dad had been born too late for the Second World War, his grandpas had got off for being teachers or doing something vital at steelworks, and all the miners seemed to avoid it too. But here *was* a hero – a brother of his great grandmother on his mother's side, who had joined up at the age of seventeen and sailed from Devonport to Suez in December 1914, then over to France. He would have stopped briefly here in Amiens – they threw tins of bully beef to children in the streets. Then began their march to Colincamps and the front, via a series of billets in French farms. The battalion entered the trenches on the 3rd of April 1915, opposite the Germans at Serre; he died in that hell of the first of July.

Joe had hitched a lift the next day in a van as far as the town of Albert with a man who stank authentically of stale sweat and Camel cigarettes. He could have hired a car but this was more of an adventure: more 'French' – something Sonia would never have let him do if she'd been here – he'd best not tell her when he got back.

'Je pay un visite à la monument de Thiepval,' he had said to the man; 'Le frère de ma grand grand mère est là. Je cherche le nom. Il est mort le premier Juillet.'

The man had rabbitted on and he had only caught the odd word here and there, something about his own grandpère and Verdun, something about Angela Merkel. Joe replied with a few "oui"s and "c'est sûr"s which seemed to work. The man shook his hand when they got to Albert and insisted on buying him a huge beer: "un formidable" he had called it: "J'aime les Anglais, moi," he'd said. Joe, somewhat embarrassed at the fuss, and slightly anxious that the man was coming on to him, wished he had kept up his French. He felt he retrieved the situation when he raised his glass and drained it to: "L'entente cordiale!"

His head had throbbed as he walked along those roads in the sun; yellow waving fields, peaceful and shimmering in the sun. He thought he heard echoes of guns and cries of extinguished manhood. Wrong time of year for poppies, alas.

Here it was so quiet, so still; swallows flying low over the well-tended grass. He took off his cap as he stared up at the arch – more awesome than beautiful. "Here are recorded names of officers and men of the British Armies who fell on the Somme battlefields between July 1915 and March 1918 but to whom the fortune of war denied the known and honoured burial given to their comrades in death."

Up there amongst those seventy six thousand names was that of Ironside, A – one hero among many.

On his own two hour march to the front, the eight or

so kilometres down empty lanes from Albert, his Ray-Bans on, with Elgar's cello concerto on his iPod, he had imagined what he would have felt as a nineteen-year-old taking that same journey that Alf had; fixing his bayonet, following his pals up the ladder to what he must have feared was his certain heroic death.

Looking up at the names, a proud tear rolled down his cheek which he would not brush away. To them we owe so much.

Sonia, gorgeous, infuriating Sonia, should have come with him; it would have been more fun if she had. "You go and walk amongst your ghosts," she had said as she stuffed clothes into a suitcase. "It's obvious you'd rather be with them than me. I'm going to Gwyndy with Sue and her kids." He had planned it badly: dropping his plans on her at the last minute, but once he had got the idea of coming here in his head it was something he had to do – for Alf.

"What is the bloody point of it all, eh Joe? All you've got is a big piece of paper with names on it. You spend more time with your dead relatives than you do with your living ones – or me. It's not even like you know anything about them really: it's all in your head. What's wrong with here and now?"

He sat down on the grass with the sun on his back, got out his lunch and Wilfred Owen out of his pocket. It was her loss. Wet Wales – or sunshine, brioche, a crottin de chèvre and cannettes of blonde! He'd bring her back a bottle of Calvados; she'd soon come round.

In the afternoon he would see if he could get to Colincamps, see if he could find the front line.

The peace was disturbed by his phone ringing. He looked at the screen: Sonia. He smiled.

'Hi Sonia, how's Wales, is it raining?' he laughed.

'It's not Sonia it's Sue.'

'Sue?'

'Listen Joe, I've some bad news you need to come back as quick as you can.'

The Hand Keeps Moving

Joe stepped off the train and held the package close to his chest; it was a present from Emma who told him to swear he would not open it until he arrived at his barracks.

He was 21, two years in the Army and on his first tour. The last three weeks he had been on leave and spent every minute of the day with his beloved Emma. Tomorrow he would fly out to Afghanistan, but tonight he would stay overnight at the RAF base.

'Take us to the RAF camp please mate,' he said to the taxi driver.

On arriving at the camp, he registered and then made for the barracks. The line of beds stood empty. He dropped his kit bag and threw himself onto one of the beds and eagerly started to unwrap the package. It was a leather-bound writing book and an expensive looking pen. He delicately opened the book and took the lid off the pen, and wrote, *Joe and Emma 1996.*

*

The two soldiers sat staring at their badly injured buddy in the hospital bed.

The room was sparse of any furniture, except a scratched and chipped bedside cabinet and a large wooden wall clock that made its presence known by the heavy tap of the minute hand.

'He didn't deserve this,' the soldier said, his tired eyes transfixed on his buddy.

'I know,' the other soldier replied. He was hunched over looking at a spot on the floor. He closed his eyes and rubbed his fingertips hard over his temples.

The minute hand continued to add its contribution to this solemn gathering. The clock played with the two soldiers like an owl watching its prey. It knew there was no hiding place so it continued to remind them that time was ebbing away.

'You remember the time we had leave and old soppy bollocks over there chatted up a transvestite outside that club,' the soldier said, trying his hardest to lift the mood and hold it together.

'He was never very lucky with the opposite sex was he?' his mate said, lifting his head up to reveal the many criss-cross worry lines below his eyes and a red blotchy and weather-beaten face.

The clock continued to do its job, like it had always done, cold and robotic but never a minute late.

'Well he found his true love in Emma. God, he loved that girl,' the soldier said, not taking his eyes off his injured comrade.

'Yeah, though what she saw in him! Never shut up about her – just before he got hit he was going on about how gorgeous she was,' his mate said, continuing to stare at the floor.

'Always excuses not to come down the NAAFI, so he could write his letters and poems. Romantic sod. Come on son, wake up, you've got your whole life in front of you, come on!'

The soldiers' buddy lay motionless in the bed. His eyelids were closed and slightly twitching; he looked peaceful like a baby sleeping. The short, shallow breaths sounded loud in the oxygen mask as though someone was breathing through a microphone and the sound filled the room.

'This heat is overbearing, I'll be glad to leave this

godforsaken place for good,' the soldier said, taking off his camouflage to reveal sinewy sun-tanned arms.

The other soldier followed, stripping back to his tee-shirt, then got up and peered outside the room.

'Excuse me nurse any chance of some water in here?'

The clock continued to remind the soldiers that another minute had past.

The nurse came in and delivered the water. She briefly looked at her watch and then left as quickly as she came in, as though she'd seen it all before.

The soldier poured out two cups of water and gave one to his mate. They both drained the small white plastic cups and refilled them.

'Do you think he'll come round? That was one hell of a knock he took there,' the soldier said, talking to the floor.

'He'll be all right, he's young, if it had been you or me, maybe not, but he'll pull through, he's one tough bastard.'

Life went on outside the room, the sound of voices and army trucks could be heard.

'If he doesn't pull through—'

'No ifs. He's going to make it!'

'But I can't face Emma, I don't think I can do another one; I've had three in the last six months already.'

'I know, don't worry, he isn't going to die, I'm sure of that.'

The proud-looking clock hung there, indifferent to the gravity of the situation. It had seen many young men in that same bed taken early to their graves, but it continued to strike its minute hand like it had always done and always will do.

'Come on cocker wake up, you remember that kick-about we had, us against the Royals, you got the ball and just ran, you shouted to me to get out of your way, like a man possessed. And that shot that almost took the net out. You shouted, this one's for Emma!'

'Yeah what was he on? Didn't stop running. 5-0 wasn't it?'

'I think it was more than that, I can't remember,' the soldier said, turning his head back to his injured buddy.

The sound of the clock broke the silence between the two men.

'You ever thought what you'd do if you left the Army?'

'I don't think I could do anything else, I might as well stick it out now and get the pension.'

'I think I've had enough of all this now, I'm thinking of getting out.'

'What would you do?'

'I don't know, could get a driving job I suppose, I got my HGV licence, that's one good thing I've got from the Army.'

The soldier put both hands over his face, lost in his thoughts, then in a slow circular movement rubbed both his tired eyes ploughing up the loose skin and making deep furrows in his forehead. He stared at his friend in the bed.

The clock continued to strike.

A thick atmosphere was now beginning to descend on the room, where hope and optimism does not survive.

'Yeah, I'm going to get out of the Army, I've had enough of seeing twenty-year-old lads being put in coffins. What are we fighting for anyway?'

'We're fighting for freedom, so that other people can live their lives with the choices we have.'

'That's crap, you see the way the people look at us when we're patrolling; they hate our guts and can't wait to see the back of us.'

The soldier stood up and turned away from the bed

and walked to the window. He rested his large hands on the cracked and peeling window sill; his gold band shone in the blinding sun. He could hear many voices – various accents, male and female. He put his hand to his face to hide the sun and looked out onto the large expanse of the compound. People were rushing around like a nest of ants that had just been disturbed – running in all directions shouting, gesticulating. An Army chopper was descending from the sky preparing to land. Below a team of medical orderlies waited to receive their latest casualty. The doors of the chopper flew open and army personnel rushed out with another offering.

The soldier turned away from the window and glanced at his mate who was still staring at the floor. He slowly looked around the room – the faded walls, the torn linoleum on the floor. His attention was caught by the striking clock. He studied the clock. It looked out of place, he thought to himself. He imagined it being on the wall of some exclusive Gentleman's Club, where polished wooden floors, large silver chandeliers and exquisite porcelain ornaments prevailed.

He returned to his seat and stared at his motionless buddy again. There had been no change.

'What you thinking of, eh? I bet you're thinking about Emma and what you both are going to do together when you get out of here, holiday in the sun somewhere, actually you've probably had enough of the sun, I know I certainly have. I bet you'll go skiing, just you and Emma in some lovely warm log cabin somewhere, nice glass of wine, eh? I bet that's what you'll do.'

'Yes I've definitely decided, I'm going to get out of the Army, start a new life; have more time with my family.'

The clock struck on the hour like it always did and

always will do. The two soldiers instinctively looked at one another, as though they both knew.

The breathing had stopped.

Silver Linings

You must think me a very bad person. When so many have sacrificed so much: their sons, their fathers, their brothers – their own lives. It's not that I've been untouched by all that; I've had my share, like we all have. I have grieved, but I have also been blissfully, ecstatically happy – like somehow the one balances out the other. Before the Kaiser brought his black clouds over Europe I was never, what I now know to be, happy – that unbounded joy you get when your team-mate puts in a cross, right to your feet, and you have time to look up and pick your spot before letting it fly: seeing the goalie stretch, but you know she'll never reach it, then seeing the net ripple, and the smiles on the girls' faces, and their arms around your shoulders. Before the war I smiled politely but I never, ever, shrieked with joy. It is not that my childhood was unhappy. Life was just what it was. Under my father's, then under my husband's roof.

When war came and took my husband to France, sadness was tinged with relief – no, that's not it – relief was tinged with regret. Regret for our marriage. A marriage that had disappointed both of us. I could not be a wife like his mother was: to wait for his return each day. And he was not the charming, dutiful man I thought he was. So, when I waved him off to war, I felt sorry for him. All that anger he had in him. Most of the time it was hidden. Everybody thought him the perfect gentleman – good ol' George! But it was always there – a growing pot of boiling temper, bound and constrained by decorum. And every now and then, it blew – like that steam boiler in the factory did. It built up inside him, had to find a way out, and wreaked destruction. As the train pulled away, he leaned out of the window like all the other Tommies. There was sadness in his eyes. But, as I said, my first emotion was relief. His little boy eyes would not make me behave like the other wives. I was free from fear of him returning at closing time, fear of his moods, his overpowering strength, his fists. Like that time I came back from the Women's Suffrage march in town:

'Elsie, how can you side with those awful creatures?' he said.

'But, George dear. They are just ordinary women. We only want what is right.'

'Right? Right? What's right about putting bombs in post-boxes, defacing property and defying your husband? Nothing more than bloody terrorists! Bad as Fenians!'

'They are driven to desperation. No one will listen. We've a right to our say.'

'We? *They* are set on destroying this country. Just a load of vile harridans.'

My mistake was to stand up to him. I should have just let it blow over, but I let my own emotions rule me and said:

'Is that what you think of me, George? A vile harridan?' Then he struck me.

'You behave like a whore, you deserve to be treated like one!'

He was full of remorse afterwards, he apologised and even cried. I think he genuinely was disgusted by himself. He was attentive and devoted for weeks – but it wasn't the last time. I suppose it wasn't really his fault, God rest his soul. I think his father treated him terribly as a child – he had bad blood in him.

So I became a munitionette. Me and my lathe were a team – Gertie, I called her. She was a bit temperamental –

needed coaxing along, but me and her produced twice as many shells in a day as a man ever could: because I understood her. I got the best out of her. She sang as I wound in the cutting tool: beautiful, shiny shells. Then I retrained and now I drive a huge crane called Bess. I earn good money too. It's exhausting of course, and I have broken, grimy fingernails, dirty hair and skin that never comes clean, but, at the end of every day, I've achieved something – done my bit. As well as money, I earn respect, and I'm proud of myself and my family at the works – that's what we are: one big family. Like out there on the pitch, we work together all have our own roles. We cheer each other up, sometimes we cry together when news comes from the front, but we stick together.

It was at the works I also became a footballer. This is when I truly come alive – when I run and my heart pounds and my blood courses through my veins and my lungs feel like they'll burst in the cold air. Out there on the pitch next to the works, we share something magical – we are a team of strong women. We work together and we become stronger than just eleven.

At first, Mr Grimes despaired as we all ran around the ball in an undisciplined gaggle. He even shouted from the sidelines: "You are not geese chasing a meal bucket!" Back then there was more laughter than effort, but now we form combinations and stick to our roles: each part of the machine performing its function. We've learnt to push the ball out to the wings, not just to rush straight for goal in a one-woman dash. And old Mr Grimes had his blackboard out again on Saturday, drawing circles and arrows, and it is starting to make sense: even off-side.

We are in the South Yorkshire Ladies' Football League,

and in with a chance of winning the end-of-season Fifty Guinea Cup which is awarded to the winners, provided we can overcome the Vickers' girls. Last week we beat the Empire Mills team at Barnsley and Mr Grimes said he was proud of the way we came back from behind, but, what is more important, we were proud of ourselves. In the Christmas holidays we played the National Projectile Factory at Bramall Lane. Can you believe it? There were thousands there to watch us. Not that you'd know it from the newspapers. You never see our results in the paper; like we don't exist. Some things never change. You see every junior result and every men's league result going. I even wonder if they think we'll go away if they just ignore us.

We footballers get special treatment in the works' canteen, as well; though no one ever says. I've noticed Addie slip an extra chunk or two of meat into my bowl with a little smile – like she's doing her bit for the team she comes along to support.

So, you can see why I have never been as happy as now. Do you think that makes me a bad person? When the war comes to an end, as it surely must soon, I have got to hang on to some of this. Of course the works will close. There will be no more canteen, no social evenings, no camaraderie – and our team will fold. But I have got to do something fulfilling. Women will be heard. And I have got to play football – it has become such a part of me.

In 1921 the old-school-tie codgers of the FA banned women from playing on football grounds under their auspices because: "…the game of football is quite unsuitable for females and ought not to be encouraged."

About the Authors

<u>Steven Kay</u>

Steve published his first novel, *The Evergreen in red and white* independently in early 2014. It was long-listed for the Historical Novel Society's 2015 Indie awards. It is based on the true story of Rabbi Howell, the first Romani footballer and his struggles to do the right thing, constrained by the morals of a northern Victorian town and torn between two women.

He has also indie-published three, out-of-print classics and a short story collection. He has recently set up an authors' network: www.sheffieldauthors.co.uk to support and showcase local authors, and is working on novels three and four and other publications—in between his 9 to 5 distraction from writing.
www.1889books.co.uk, twitter:@SteveK1889 ,
http://stevek1889.blogspot.co.uk/

<u>Elizabeth Thomas</u>

Elizabeth submitted her first short story *Home* for judging in a competition in 2014 and received a special commendation from the judges. Having enjoyed the writing process, Elizabeth's enthusiasm to produce more short stories on a similar theme inspired this collection. Elizabeth is currently writing her debut novel. Elizabeth can be contacted at: elizabeththomas@live.com.

<u>Clare Coombes</u>

Clare writes psychological thrillers and historical fiction.

Her debut novel *Definitions*, a psychological thriller based in Liverpool, was released by Bennion Kearny in 2015. Clare has also been published and commended for her short stories and novel extracts in a number of publications, including the Writers' Forum, the Fish Short Memoir Prize, Subtext Magazine, The Lancashire Evening Post, Know Magazine and various academic journals. She was a finalist in the Writing on the Wall Pulp Idol contest, leading to publication in the anthology *Pulp Idol Firsts 2014*. She has a Masters in Writing from Liverpool John Moores University and a degree in English Literature from the University of Liverpool. Clare is also a writer for Liverpool John Moores University, covering science and technology research for international, national and local media. She is currently working on a novel combining the genres of psychological thriller and historical fiction. This follows the story of two teenagers who meet on the run from pre-war Nazi Germany, and explores the effects of their upbringing and years of indoctrination on their relationship as they fall in love. It is set to form part of a trilogy. *The Girl and the Boy on the Train* in this anthology is an adaption of one of the chapters.

www.clare-coombes.com, twitter: @coombes_clare

Leela Soma

Leela Soma was born in Madras, India and now lives in Glasgow. Her poetry and short stories have been published in a number of anthologies and publications, including The Scotsman, The Grind, New Voices and Gutter magazine. She won the Margaret Thomson Davis Trophy for her novel *Twice Born*. (2008) Her second novel *Bombay Baby* was published by Dahlia Publishing Limited in 2011. *Boxed In* a short story collection e-book was published by The Pot Hole Press in 2013. She was commissioned along with 21 other writers and artists to write a story for Glasgow Women's Library anthology *21 Revolutions* for its 21st birthday in 2013. Her latest story is in the anthology, launched on August 7th 2015, *Butterfly Rammy* a commissioned short story for the Edinburgh Fringe show 2015.

She is working on her third novel; the main character is Inspector Patel, a crime fiction set in Glasgow's West End. She has served on the committee for the Milngavie Books and Arts

Festivals and on the Scottish Writer's Centre Committee. Her work reflects her dual heritage of India and Scotland. www.leelasoma.com, twitter: @Glasgowlee,

Elizabeth Phillips Scott

Elizabeth is a graduate from the RSAMD now called the Royal conservatoire. She graduated in 1984 and worked in professional theatre and TV until her mother fell ill and she had to return home. She started writing poetry when very young and has had poems published in Forward. She wrote a play in the 80's with Caroline Patterson called Hejab and the lift man that was directed by Andy Mackie and performed by her and Caroline at the festival at the little royal lyceum. She has various writing projects on the go and a detective drama called *A Stab in the Dark*.

Kristy Kerruish

Kristy was born in Edinburgh and currently lives in The Netherlands. She is by trade a historian, publishing under her maiden name. She writes fiction and poetry and has recently had work placed in Dream Catcher, Spelk Fiction, Winamop, Dawntreader and Gold Dust among others. *Silence* is based on a relative's account of the blitz.

Kevan Youde

Kevan was born in Derbyshire and has spent most of his professional career in Europe, working as a marine scientist and writing fiction in his spare time. He has had work selected recently for publication in Dream Catcher, Bunbury and Spelk Fiction among others. *Barriers & Bombs* is based on a family member's account of the bombings in Liverpool.

Cheryl Jennifer Hubbard

Cheryl has been writing ever since she could hold a pen in her hand and understand words to write. After a career in retail she has taken the plunge and become a mature student at Chichester University doing a three year degree in English and Writing.

Kevin Crowe

Kevin was born in Manchester in 1951, and has worked as a factory worker, barman, youth worker and social worker. In 1999, he and his partner moved to Durness in the Highlands to open a bookshop and restaurant. They retired in 2015. In 2005, he and Simon became the first gay couple in the Highlands to enter a civil partnership and in 2014 married. He has had poetry, fiction, reviews and essays published in magazines, websites and anthologies, and has appeared on radio and TV. He is a regular contributor to the Highland magazines *Am Bratach*, the online LGBT magazine *UnDividing Lines* and the online LGBT magazine and news feed *KaleidoScot*. He was a founder member of North West Highland Writers and is convenor of the Highland LGBT Writers Group. Until recently he was on the committee of Highland LGBT Forum and a tutor on the Pink Castle Philosophy Club. He currently lives in Wick in the North Highlands with his husband Simon. His Facebook page is: Kevin.crowe.775

Frances MacArthur

Frances is a retired English teacher who has written 6 crime novels. She lives on the south side of Glasgow, alone since her husband died in 2013. She likes holidaying in the Far East.

Frances' other work can be found on her Amazon page.

Phil Carter

Phil is originally from Abingdon, Oxfordshire. However, he has spent the majority of his life living in various parts of London, and now resides in Surrey, where he has the great pleasure of walking and cycling around the Surrey Hills.

He writes short stories. For further information please contact: philcarter1965@yahoo.co.uk

Caroline Cannons

Caroline was brought up in care in Nottingham. After gaining an Honours degree in Education at Sheffield

University, she taught French in Kent secondary schools for over thirty years. Retiring from her post as deputy head teacher in 2012, she returned to university and studied creative writing, Her first story was published a year later. Founder member of *The Canterbury Yarners*, she reads her work to audiences at festivals and writing groups within Kent.

twitter: @cannons47,
https://penscratch8309.wordpress.com/2015/12/29/dear-cynthia/

Sarah Oakes

Originally from Letchworth Garden City, Hertfordshire. Sarah is in her first year at university, studying English and Creative Writing at the University of Chichester. Her short story in this selection: *All the Same* is her first short story to be published (so far!)

Mark J Howard

Mark is a 50 year old homeless Lancastrian who nevertheless loves life and enjoys writing. He says: "When we stop spending uncounted billions on war, nobody need be homeless or hungry again. It's not rocket surgery, is it?" Another of Mark's stories and a short interview can be found at:
http://stevek1889.blogspot.co.uk/2015/02/nicks-game-short-story-by-mark-j-howard.html

Joy Nwosu Lo-Bamijoko

Joy was born and grew up in Enugu, Nigeria, a beautiful

town nestled in hills. She moved to Italy, and spent ten years in Rome, studying and waiting out the end of the civil war, returning to Lagos in 1972 as a radio producer, then as a university lecturer. She has a Ph.D. in Music Education from the University of Michigan and moved to New Jersey in 1996, where she was a school teacher. Since retiring in 2008 she has lived between Lagos, New Jersey and Los Angeles. Her work includes: *Mirror of Our Lives: Voices of Four Igbo Women*, shortlisted for the Commonwealth Book Contest in 2012, and *The Legend of the Walking Dead: Igbo Mythologies*.

If you want some idea of what Ijeoma's singing might have been like, download the music of Joy Nwosu and her Group, recorded in the 1970s (yes, she is annoyingly multi-talented!).

twitter: @Jinlobify,

http://sbprabooks.com/JoyNwosuLoBamijoko/